FROM USA TODAY BESTSELLING AUTHOR
ERIN BEDFORD

LOVED BY THE Vampires

HOUSE OF DURAND
BOOK SIX

Also by Erin Bedford

The Underground Series
Chasing Rabbits
Chasing Cats
Chasing Princes
Chasing Shadows
Chasing Hearts
The Crimes of Alice
Hatter's Heart

The Mary Wiles Chronicles
Marked by Hell
Bound by Hell
Deceived by Hell
Tempted by Hell

Starcrossed Dragons
Riding Lightning
Grinding Frost
Swallowing Fire
Pounding Earth

The Crimson Fold
Until Midnight
Until Dawn
Until Sunset

Curse of the Fairy Tales
Rapunzel Untamed
Rapunzel Unveiled

Her Angels
Heaven's Embrace
Heaven's A Beach
Heaven's Most Wanted

ERIN BEDFORD

LOVED BY THE Vampires

HOUSE OF DURAND
BOOK SIX

Chapter 1

Piper

I COULD JUST MOVE next Thursday's meeting to the following Monday…and there. I smacked enter on my keyboard with a resounding clack. I was done for the weekend.

With a long sigh of relief, I logged out of my computer and pushed back from my desk. Working for a lawyer wasn't the most exciting job, especially not when your previous employment included so much excitement it almost killed you. Multiple times. But it was better than sitting around the house waiting for the others to tell me we could go back to our regular lives.

"You out of here for the day, Piper?" Bethany, a curly red-headed paralegal, smiled down at me as she stopped at my desk. In a tight, formfitting, forest green dress, the slit between the square neckline showed off just a hint of cleavage. With her perfectly on point makeup, Bethany looked the part of a serious but sexy businesswoman.

Unlike me.

I had to work twice as hard to look like more than just the plain Jane around the office. I had to admit, as much as I hated some of the outfits the Durands put me in, at least they had good taste. The best I could come up with were a series of blouses all of the same style but in different colors. I mixed and matched them with black skirts, pants, and sensible shoes. You couldn't pay me to don those death contraptions Bethany wore to work every day. She didn't have the same issues I did though. I never knew when I might need to run.

Holding back disdain from the way my thoughts had turned, I opened my desk drawer and grabbed my purse. "Yep. Right this moment." My eyes darted to the open door of our boss' office, Jack Biggs. I lowered my voice. "If I can get by the Big Man." We both rolled our eyes and giggled quietly. Jack Biggs was just as arrogant as his last name. In his opinion, no one was better than Jack Biggs. Not in the courtroom…or the bedroom, which he'd not so subtly slipped into the conversation not even the first week I'd been working for him.

"It's hard to believe you've been working here a year." Bethany bumped my arm with hers as we walked toward the exit. Her heels clicked on the tiled floor, unfortunately signaling the Big Man of our departure.

"Piper!"

I held my answer to Bethany and cursed under my breath. Giving her an exasperated look before spinning around, I forced a smile on my face. "Mr. Biggs, I was just heading out. What can I do for you?"

"Please, Piper. How many times have I told you to call me Jack?" The dimple in his cheek peeked out as his full lips curved up in a flirtatious grin. Some people would be orgasming over having a boss like Jack Biggs. He had black hair that was almost blue in a certain light, and warm brown eyes that his smiles actually reached. If I was any other woman, I would have been delighted to have him as a boss, let alone someone interested in me, but I had more than my fair share of beautiful men, and frankly, Jack didn't hold a candle to them.

Clutching my purse strap tighter, I glanced over at Bethany who was holding back a smile. Inwardly, I groaned. On the outside, I gave a polite chuckle. "At least one more time, Mr. Biggs. Did you need something? I'd really like to get home."

"No, you're not!" Bethany gasped and smacked me on the arm. "This is your one year at the company. We have to go out and celebrate. Come on, Jack, tell her!" Bethany turned her pouty lips toward Jack and fluttered her long lashes over her big hazel eyes. As much as Jack was interested in me, Bethany was far more interested in him. She once told me she wanted to have his Biggy babies. Really. She said it exactly like that. I wanted to vomit. A little like the way I felt now at the prospect of going out to celebrate my one-year workiversary.

To them, it might seem like a momentous occasion. But to me, it reminded me that I was dying a little bit inside each day that went by. Instead of voicing what I really thought of going out with them, I shoved down all my emotions that were billowing up and put on a strong face.

"I really shouldn't. I need to—" I tried to make my excuses, but Jack interrupted me.

"You are the best receptionist I've ever had. You don't have any work you need to do. And I know for sure that your boss would approve." He winked at me, causing Bethany to giggle.

Seeing that I was not getting out of this, I conceded, "Fine. One drink." I held my finger up with a stern look. "Just one."

"That's my girl!" Bethany cheered, and looped her arm through mine as they steered me out of the building.

With my free hand, I grabbed my phone and shot a quick text to Darren to let him know I was going out. There was a fifty-fifty chance he wouldn't even look at it.

Darren had taken up the head of the household role quite easily since we went into hiding. Or rather the Durands had. Darren and I were playing at being normal humans for the time being. That time seeming to be endless since we'd first moved to Seabrick a year ago. I'd hoped it would be short-lived. My promise to not wait around for them hadn't quite gone as planned. Hard to bust down the doors of the vampire hunters when you had no idea how to find them. Plus, I might be a human servant, but that only allotted me so many extra benefits.

Speed, heightened senses, and unfortunately, raging hormones. Darren kept telling me they would get under control eventually, but I had yet to see it.

"So, where are we going?" I asked, trying to keep my mind off my own tragic life, and focused on my pretend one.

"Just down a block or two." Jack pointed to the west once we stepped out of the building. Seabrick was a cute little town with a fifteen-minute walk to the beach from any part of town. I guessed that was why Antoine had planned for Darren and me to go here. No vampire in their right mind would live by the beach, where getting as much sun as possible was the motivation for practically all its residents.

There wasn't a pale face in sight as we walked down the street. Everyone had a nice tan from—if not spending time on the beach—being outside in general. And they were all just so...happy. It was sickening really. Who was that happy? There had to be something in the water.

"Were you able to move my meeting?" Jack glanced over at me, his long legs having to shorten their stride to keep in line with Bethany and myself.

Thankful for something non-personal to talk about, I offered him a small smile. "Yes. I moved it to Monday."

Jack grimaced. "Not too early, I hope?"

I suppressed a giggle. "Of course not. We wouldn't want the Big Man to lose any beauty sleep, would we?"

Jack smirked as Bethany groaned.

"You're not seriously going to talk about work this whole time, are you? This is a celebration!" Bethany skipped a bit in her three-inch heels, jerking me with her. "I want to know more about you, Piper."

"Me?" I squeaked, my shoulders bunching up at the idea of spilling all my secrets.

"You've been here a year now and we hardly know anything about you," Bethany continued with a disappointed frown.

"That's not true," I argued, avoiding both of their astute gazes. I hadn't been very forthcoming with information, because trying to lie to a lawyer was like taking a polygraph test on steroids. On top of never being good at hiding my thoughts on my face—something Rayne didn't need his powers to see—it was near impossible for me to tell my coworkers anything without giving away my double life.

"Okay, fine. We know you're from a small town outside of Atlanta. You have a mom and a dad who you don't speak to much. You're not married. No kids. And your favorite color is a pale crystal-like blue, but not like the sky, almost white."

I stared at her for a long moment. "You remember all that?"

Jack chuckled. "She's not my paralegal for nothing. Bethany has a memory like a steel trap." He tapped the side of his head with a proud grin. "You say it, she remembers it."

Bethany beamed at Jack as we stopped before one of a dozen bars in Seabrick. For a place as small as it was, they sure liked to drink.

Jack held the door open for us and we walked into The Croaking Parrot. While it was named after the colorful bird, the inside of the bar was the complete opposite. Dark wood covered the floor, the walls, and even the bar top. The only color that filled the place was the mismatched barstools ranging from cold silver metal, to bright orange and red plastic, and a multitude of different woods. The only thing that did match were the tables spread throughout the rest of the bar's interior.

I'd wonder why the owner would call it The Croaking Parrot, except there were tons of pictures on the walls of different parrots, or maybe it was the same parrot in different places? Hell if I knew. They all looked the same to me. A creepy stuffed parrot sat behind the bar on the shelf next to the mirror-backed shelves.

Freaky.

The place already bustled with happy hour nine to fivers, ready to get their weekend drink on. We were lucky to find three stools next to each other at the bar in the crowded room. Bethany obviously hoped Jack would sit next to her, but we ended up with me in the middle of the two of them. I could already feel myself needing that drink.

"What are you having?" The bartender was a pretty, alternative looking woman with shaggy pink and green hair, with one side hanging down over half of her face and the other side of her head buzzed. An array of earrings lined the visible ear. They went along well with the brow, nose, and lip piercings. I itched to ask her if she ever had trouble getting through airport metal detectors.

"I'll have a Cosmo," Bethany chirped, beaming at the woman, picking a very businesswoman drink.

"Whatever you have on tap is fine." Jack inclined his head toward the beers.

"And you?" The bartender stared hard at me with a less than thrilled attitude.

I shifted in my seat, not sure what I wanted to drink. I could tell the bartender was getting irritated by my hesitation, but before I could answer, a warm arm wrapped around my shoulders, pulling me back against a familiar chest as a smooth, no-nonsense voice told the bartender, "She'll have wine. White. No Riesling. And make it two." The bartender left with a nod to fill our order while Bethany gasped.

"Oh, my. Who is this gorgeous piece of eye candy? You have been holding out on me, Piper." She gave me a chastising look as she giggled and blushed at the man behind me.

"Do you know this man?" Jack questioned with a bit of stiffness to his voice.

I placed my hand over the arm around me and leaned back against him. "Yes, this is Darren. My boyfriend."

"You have a boyfriend?" Bethany's eyes bugged out of her head and her mouth dropped before she clipped it shut and gave me a knowing look. "Now I know why you never talked about your home life. I wouldn't want to tell anyone about someone who looked like him."

Darren's arm tightened around me, not because he was uncomfortable with her

16

words, he'd had worse said to him by creatures who wanted to do more than drool over him. I hoped one day I'd have that easy of a reaction to someone talking about me like I wasn't there. Unfortunately, my mouth and temper seemed to be the cause of a lot of my issues with the Durands. Sad but true.

Thankfully, Darren answered for me. "We prefer to keep our business and personal lives separate."

"Is that so?" Jack directed the question toward me, suspicion beginning to creep into his voice.

I dipped my head and pretended to be bashful. "Uh, yeah."

"Is that who you were texting?" Bethany asked, finally getting over her surprise.

The bartender came back and handed out the drinks. I took a sip of mine with a sigh. "Yeah."

"That's so sweet." Bethany giggled and drank from her Cosmo. "How long have you two been together?"

I twisted in my seat so my back was to the bar and I wasn't having to split my attention between the three of them. "A few years now." I sipped from my glass as I met Darren's dark eyes. He quirked a brow at me, but didn't argue.

It had taken two months before I could get Darren to stop wearing his butler suit. He'd even conceded the gloves after I'd pestered him for a whole day about them. We weren't working with vampires now. At least, not face to face. It took a while to get used to Darren in jeans. Even now I had to do a double-take sometimes. If Darren in a suit was delicious, then Darren in tight-fitting denim was practically sinful.

"And what do you do, Darren no last name?" Jack inquired with more prejudice than I expected from my boss.

"It's Pritchard," Darren supplied, his eyes not leaving mine.

"And what do you do?"

I shot a look at Bethany at Jack's line of questioning. She shrugged, no more clued into what our boss was thinking. He was acting like an overprotective boyfriend, but not in the attractive 'I think I have a claim on her and want to know what she sees in you' kind of way.

Antoine.

He sounded like Antoine. The thought of the head of the house of Durand made my heart ache, and Darren took my hand in his, directing my attention back to him. He always seemed to know when I was thinking of our vampire master. Not that I'd ever call

Antoine master to his face. He'd have a field day with that. Antoine was arrogant enough.

Darren held my gaze for a long moment before turning to Jack. "I'm a liaison for a high-profile family overseas."

Jack's brows rose. He took a swig from his beer and twisted it on the top of the bar. "And what exactly does that entail?"

Something in Darren shifted, and as if he were reading from a script as he responded, "I handle the household issues, run errands, and do *anything* the family needs to keep running smoothly."

"So...you're an assistant?" Bethany jutted her glass toward Darren.

Darren's lips ticked up at the side, his eyes sparkling with amusement. "Of a sort."

"And you two...live together?" Bethany shifted a finger between the two of us.

"Uh, yeah. For a while now." I drank deeply from my glass, letting the alcohol soothe my nerves. Too many more questions and I'd be spilling my guts about the whole damn thing.

"That's curious." Jack hummed, though I could tell he was holding back what he really wanted to say. I worked with the man five days a week. Jack rarely held his tongue, but for some reason this time he did.

Either way, I was glad for it. I didn't want to know what Darren would do if Jack tried to get in his face about it. The butler had dealt with vampires far longer than any of us three have been alive. A puny human man was nothing to him.

"Why?" Darren retorted, and I tightened my hand on his.

What the hell was he doing?

Did he want to start a fight?

"Why what?" Jack met Darren's challenging gaze.

"Why is that curious?"

I gave a nervous chuckle and patted Darren on the chest. "Jack's just being polite. He speaks lawyerese. Don't try to understand it."

"No." Darren's expression and tone went flat as he stared Jack down. "I do believe he means something else entirely. Don't you, Jack?"

My eyes skittered to Bethany, who kept her eyes on her drink, not letting herself be sucked into this pissing contest. Lucky her. Jack, on the other hand, had no problem picking up what Darren was insinuating.

"You're correct." Jack sat his beer down and turned completely toward us. "I find it peculiar that Piper has worked as my receptionist for a year now and not once mentioned a boyfriend, let alone one she lives with."

"As he said, we're—" I tried to interrupt him, but Jack turned his accusations onto me.

"He's not even your emergency contact. How can he be your boyfriend? You have your mother written down. That seems a bit off to me, doesn't it, Bethany?"

Bethany waved a hand at the bartender. "Another please. And keep them coming." To Jack, she shook her head. "Nope. Nothing seems off to me."

"You are a suspicious man, Jack." Darren stepped closer to me, his hands on my hips. If he were a dog, he'd be pissing on my leg to mark his territory.

"It comes with the job, Darren." Jack stood, his six-foot frame giving him the advantage over Darren's five-ten. "My nose can pick up a lie in seconds and you two reek of bullshit."

I gaped at my boss. "Excuse me." I jumped out of my seat and placed my glass down on the bar, putting myself between the two of them. "You might be my boss, but my personal life is none of your damn business. Nor who my emergency contact is. I came out with you guys against my better judgment and this is how you act?" I huffed and shoved my purse over my shoulder. "I've had enough employers pushing the limits of our work relationship, and I won't be pushed by you. Now, if you'll excuse me. I'm going home. I'll see you Monday. If you still wish to keep me as your receptionist, that is."

Jack gaped at me and then hurried to say, "Of course I do. I didn't mean to—"

"Good," I interjected, and grabbed Darren's arm. "Let's go. Bethany, I'll see you later."

"Bye." She waved meekly before burying her face back into her drink. I bet she was regretting dragging me to drinks now. She could pay for our drinks then as an apology.

Marching us out of the bar, I clenched my teeth and held my anger until we were all the way home. A feat in itself for me.

However, the moment we stepped into the quaint, two-bedroom house we'd taken up residence in, I turned on Darren, shoving my finger in his face. "What the hell was that?"

Darren laced his hands behind his back, his expression dry and without emotion. "Your employer wants to bed you."

"No fucking duh," I growled, wanting to pull my hair out. "I think I could figure that bit out for myself without you antagonizing him. Why can't you just be like you are with the vampires and not start shit?"

"We're not with vampires now." Darren took the few steps toward me until I was forced to back up as well. My back hit the wall and his arms caged me in on either side. "And it is my job to keep you safe. That includes from over interested lawyers, who think to take what doesn't belong to them."

My annoyance at Darren shifted at his nearness. My heart rate sped up and my nipples hardened as his chest brushed against my front. "And who exactly do I belong to?" I licked my lips, my mouth going dry from the intensity of his stare.

Darren leaned down, one hand brushing my blonde hair over my shoulder. "I think you know."

I shivered as his fingers trailed along my cheek and cupped the back of my neck. The relationship dynamic between Darren and myself had shifted at some point over the last year. Of course, it had already been well on its way after the scene with Antoine in his office when he'd been trying to get me to back out of going to Club Dead. However, after a year of living together, make-believing we were playing house while we waited for the vampires in our lives to outrun or kill the hunters chasing them had somehow morphed into something real. I could almost pretend like we were a normal couple just living our lives, except for the monthly visits from one of the Durands.

"Stop worrying so much," Darren murmured, brushing his lips against mine. "That's my job."

"And what's mine?" I smiled against his lips, my fingers coming up to curl into the front of his shirt. I knew I was driving him crazy by wrinkling up the material. His analness was one of the things I loved about him. Every inch of me just itched to mess up his perfectly coiffed appearance and he might be annoyed by it, but he also loved every moment of it.

Darren's other arm moved down my back, cupping my ass before finding the edge of my skirt, dipping his hand beneath it until he found my center. I gasped and bucked my hips against his touch. "You are meant to be savored and adored. Worrying does not suit the goddess that you are."

My cheeks ached with how wide I grinned. "You're such a charmer. I can see why Antoine—" Darren flicked his thumb against my clit, making me groan.

"No more talking." Darren captured my lips, devouring every inch of my mouth with his tongue. I dragged my nails through his hair and let out a grunt of annoyance as he removed his hand from between my thighs, pulling my leg up and over his hip. Rolling my hips, I ground myself against his hardness, seeking out some kind of release for the ache he had stirred in my core.

"Now, please," I gasped into his mouth, reaching between us to pull down his zipper. My hand wrapped around Darren's length, hot and hard in my grasp. He hissed at the contact. Grabbing me beneath both legs, Darren pulled me closer so my skirt bunched up at my waist. As he sank inside me, my head fell back against the wall.

In a town I didn't want to be in, away from home and everyone I knew, helpless to save the men who I'd begun to refer to as family, this was the only thing that made sense. This right here. With Darren, who had started out a reluctant coworker, and had turned into a friend, a confidant, and now lover. Calling him my boyfriend had been putting it simply, but as Darren had once explained to me his relationship with Antoine, ours was so much...more. Boyfriend didn't quite cut it. Especially when I technically had five others, if I could still call them that seeing as we only got to see each other once a month, and not even all of them together. Last time was Marcus's turn. This time was...

I pulled my mouth away from Darren's and blinked rapidly, barely able to think, let alone speak with him inside me. "What...what day is it?"

"What?" Darren grunted, his hips shifting to press even deeper inside me.

White spots formed behind my eyes and my fingers clenched into his hair as I cried out. For a moment, I lost my train of thought, absorbed by the feeling of Darren within me.

Forcing myself to think clearly, I grabbed Darren's face between my hands. "What day is it?"

"Friday, you know that." Darren cupped my ass so tightly I knew I'd have bruises tomorrow. For someone who bottomed for a vampire master, he had no issue in being the top in ours.

"No, no. The date." I smacked his shoulder and felt myself clench around him. A wave of pleasure surged through me, fogging my mind and making me forget what I was even talking about. Darren seemed overcome with the same need as he drove into me faster. With one hand, he ripped my shirt open, exposing my bra, and I couldn't get out of my clothes fast enough.

My bra went next, tossed with my shirt into the darkened house. My skirt stayed up around my waist as Darren dropped my legs and turned me around, backing me toward our couch. Bending me over the arm of the sofa, he pushed back inside me all at once. I cried out at the sudden intrusion, but then braced myself on the cushions. I didn't question our sudden ferocity, my mind focused on one thing—finding my release.

With my clit pressed against the rigid material of the couch, it didn't take long for my insides to tighten around Darren, and I screamed my release until my throat ached. Darren grunted shortly after, spilling himself inside me before slumping against my back.

While my body cooled, I took in slow, deep breaths. Having orgasmed, I could think again. What was it I was worried about again? It was then that I felt the eyes on us.

My head slowly turned toward the armchair as the lamplight clicked on.

Ebony hair tumbled over wide shoulders, his piercing blue eyes staring straight into my soul as his luscious lips curled into a devilish grin. "Well, isn't this interesting."

Fuck.

Chapter 2

Wynn

I HAD THOUGHT OF nothing more than to get back to see Piper after all this time. I'd only seen her once before over this last year, and it had been too short of a visit for anything other than a long night of passion mixed in with some tension between her and Darren.

At the time, I thought it had been the whole vampire hunter on the run situation. Piper hadn't pretended to be okay with being shoved here while we were out running around. She had been more than vocal and none of us have been able to make her feel better about it. Not even Rayne.

Antoine said she will get over it. With time. After all, we had so much time. However, now I was less sure about her getting over it than her being too comfortable where she was. With Darren.

"Wynn." Piper scowled, shifting out from under Darren and grabbing Darren's discarded shirt to cover herself. "That was fucked up, even for you. What are you doing here?"

I let my lips quirk up as I skimmed my gaze over her bare legs, the scent of arousal still filling the air. "I do believe that I have answered the question you have been asking the entire time that our attractive young Darren was, how do the young folk say it nowadays?" I held back a chuckle as Piper narrowed her eyes on me. "Taking you to pound town?"

Piper's nose scrunched up. "No one says that...like, at all."

Darren made a sound in his throat that was close to a laugh. Something I rarely heard from the stoic, well-mannered man. In fact, seeing him so uninhibited with Piper was like seeing a unicorn. He was never so willing to be mussed up by anyone, even Antoine. Piper, though, had been all over him, her hands in his hair, ripping at his clothes, and he didn't even seem to care. In fact, it seemed to get him off faster.

It was very...interesting.

"Still, I am surprised that you don't have our visits on your phone." I lifted mine up and showed where I had noted today's visit. "Are you so content with your life here," I gestured around the small but welcoming house, holding back a sniff of distaste, "working as a puffed up lawyer's assistant that you have forgotten all about us, my pet?"

Piper's back stiffened and her arms crossed over her chest as she glowered at me. Those eyes were so fierce and lethal that had I not been immortal, I might have feared for my life. My kitten had claws after all.

With heavy steps, she sauntered over to me, kicking me in the shin with a barefoot. "I'm not the one who ditched us here to go off vampire hunter...hunting."

I grinned as she flushed from her words.

Propping my arm up on the chair, I leaned my face into my palm. I could feel the wickedness sliding up my face as I contemplated the ordeal we were in. My brothers and I were unable to stand still while our loyal butler seduced the girl we were all in love with. It was indeed a plot twist none of us saw coming.

"I apologize if you have been forlorn since we have been running for our lives. If I had known how aggrieved you would be, I would have insisted we bring you along. Or at least visit more often." I uncrossed my legs, and in a single quick movement, pulled Piper into my lap. Darren, who had put on his pants—more for Piper's benefit, I was sure, than mine—gave us a once over before discretely leaving the room. I sometimes wished Piper had the same kind of decorum. Then again, I wouldn't want to sleep with her and her smart mouth if that were the case.

"You're an asshole." Piper smacked my chest with a frown and tried to stand up, but I held her in place. "You can't just walk into *our* house." She tried to stand up again. I tugged her back to me. With an aggravated sigh, she threw her hands up. "You don't live here. Darren and I do."

"Ah." I pinched her chin between my fingers and drew her face close. "But *we* own it."

This time Piper gave me a wicked grin. "No. Actually, you don't."

My lips dropped into a frown. "What do you mean?"

Pushing out of my arms—I was so dumbfounded, I allowed it—Piper marched over to a desk by one of the walls. She dug through some papers before pulling a stapled stack out and marched it back over to me. She unceremoniously dropped it into my lap.

Eyes dropping to the stack of papers, I saw that it was the deed to the house here in Seabrick. I had a sinking feeling as I flipped through the pages and saw that not once was the Durand name mentioned in the deed. In fact, the whole thing was under Piper's name. Darren wasn't even mentioned once.

"See?" Piper tapped her finger on top of the papers. "This is my house. Not yours."

For the first time in over a hundred years, I was speechless. "Uh, how...how did you manage this? I thought your finances were—"

"A mess?" Piper beamed and lifted her chin with pride. "Surprising what having a steady income can do to your credit score and your debt. Plus, since I was hoarding your guilt payments this last year, I had plenty of money to put a sizeable down payment on it."

"They were not guilt payments," I argued in mock offense, handing her the papers. "But I do have to say, I am impressed. And should I say proud?"

Piper smiled down at me and then pushed it down, making a sad attempt at being forceful. "So get out of my house." She pointed a finger at the door as if I were a dog that might do as she commanded.

I pushed back the grin fighting its way up my face and gave Piper my best smolder. "Now, love, you don't really mean that, do you?" I played with the hemline of her/Darren's shirt. "Haven't you missed me?"

Piper smacked my hand and pretended to think about it before saying, "Nope," popping her P as she cocked her hip to one side. "I'm completely satisfied with Darren and my little receptionist job with my overly flirtatious boss." She bumped my knee with her barefoot and I caught it between my hands, massaging it gently as I pulled it into my lap.

"Wynn," Piper protested, halfheartedly trying to pull her leg away from me. "Stop it. I'm mad at you. All of you."

"Are you now?" I leaned forward and placed a kiss on the inside of her knee and then just above it, causing Piper's breath to catch. "What can I possibly do to help ease your ire? Hmm?"

As I worked my mouth up the inside of Piper's thigh, her arousal flaring each inch upward, I noticed a difference in the woman before me. I hadn't noticed it before, not from the way Darren had her bent over the couch or against the wall, but the softness in Piper's body I had come to adore was practically gone. In its place, but no less sexy, were lean and defined muscles. So much strength behind these legs that I wanted to devour every inch of her.

"Why'd you stop?" Piper pouted, her coffee-colored eyes staring down at me.

"I thought you wanted me to leave?" I hummed, my lips curling up in a coy grin.

Piper seemed to catch herself, pulling her leg away from me and crossing her arms with a forced frown on her lips. "I did. I do. I mean, fuck, Wynn." She dragged a hand through her blonde hair and sat down on the coffee table behind her. "I don't know. I'm so mad at you all right now. All year you've been gone, only popping in once a month and then popping back out of my life." She gestured her arms out wildly. "I don't even get to see all of you, only one of you at a time. I feel like my life has been shoved into a standstill while you are all doing whatever the fuck you are doing to avoid or find the hunters." She wiggled her hands with so much frustration I wanted to kiss the furrow out of her brows. "And then something happened between me and Darren...and I mean, it's not like we are hearing wedding bells or anything but..."

"You want to be with him," I supplied for her, my heart feeling heavy in my chest.

I wasn't angry. I thought I might be. Jealous even. But if anything, I was sad in a bittersweet kind of way.

If I had to lose Piper to someone, I suppose it could be worse than Darren. He was one of our closest and most loyal employees and friends. He was a part of the family. He was also a human servant and knew exactly how Piper was feeling. He could give her children, if that was what she wanted. He could marry her and go out in the sun with her. I supposed we'd have to let them go sometime. I couldn't imagine that having my brothers and I around would help them. It would only make it awkward for all of us. Not to mention the hunters were still on our asses, so we couldn't exactly stay in one place to be with them anyway.

"...and like I said, I don't know how Antoine is going to feel about it, but I'm already seeing, dating, whatever," Piper waved her hands in front of her, "the five of you. I don't think adding one more is really going to be a big deal. I just don't want—"

"Wait." I held my hand up, confusion making my face pinch. "You aren't running away with Darren?"

Piper's eyes widened and her mouth dropped. Then she laughed. Loud and long. So much so that I was worried she wasn't breathing. She slapped her leg and let out a long sigh. "Oh, God. I haven't laughed like that in a long time. I mean, I absolutely love Darren. I do." She turned her head toward the back of the house. "You hear that, stick in the mud? I love your sexy ass."

Darren chuckled from what sounded like the kitchen before the sound of his footsteps came toward us. He stopped in the doorway of the living room wearing a new shirt buttoned up and looking pristine. "I love you too. Don't shout across the house. We aren't barbarians."

Wagging her brows in his direction, Piper pulled her lower lip between her teeth before saying, "Your actions when we walked in said differently."

Darren smiled a genuine smile before his eyes dipped to me. He bowed slightly before walking back to the kitchen.

"He's happy, you know," I pointed out, unable to keep the amusement out of my voice.

"I know." Piper tucked her hair behind her ear and beamed.

"After all these years, I don't think I've ever seen Darren smile quite like that before." I leaned back in my chair and crossed my legs once more. "You're good for him." Piper snorted. "You're good for all of us."

"Well," Piper stood and sashayed across the distance between us, her fingers playing with the buttons of her shirt. "What can I say? I take pride in my work." She slid into my lap, one leg on either side of my hips.

My fingers trailed over her thighs, slipping beneath the shirt to stroke her bare hips as I resisted the urge to simply sink into her right this second. "You deserve a raise."

Her fingers threaded through my hair, tipping my head back as she leaned forward, her nose brushing against mine. "I'll take it in fringe benefits." Somehow, without me noticing it, her hand had found its way into the front of my pants and grasped me in her soft grip.

Arching into her touch, I cupped the side of her face, bringing her lips to mine. "Believe me, the pleasure is all mine."

Piper's laughter was the best sound I'd heard all year. God, we needed to get rid of the hunters. I didn't know how much more

of the running I could take. Or Piper either,
for that matter.

38

Chapter 3

Piper

SWEAT DRIPPED DOWN MY heated skin, drenching the neck of my sports bra. I grunted and twisted to the side just before my trainer, Billy, could nail me in the stomach with his foot. Swinging my arm as I came out of the spin, I caught Billy on the back of the head, knocking him several feet forward.

"Damn, Piper." Billy rubbed the back of his dark bald head, his bright white teeth laughing as he held back a wince. "You don't pull any punches. Or kicks."

I took up a new fighting stance and smirked, my hands up and ready. "I thought that was the point."

Billy shook his head and held his hand up. "Hold on, supergirl. You might have unnatural human stamina, but some of us mere mortals need a break and water."

"I don't know what you mean. I have normal stamina." I relaxed my stance while Billy walked to the nearby bench to grab his water bottle. "I'm just more motivated than you are."

He grinned around the mouth of the bottle, his dark brown eyes crinkling at the edges. Swallowing and letting out a satisfied "ah," Billy pushed the top of the bottle, closing it before tossing it into his gym bag. "Yeah, well, excuse me for not wanting to hit such a pretty face."

I held back an eye roll. Billy might flirt, but he was harmless. Nothing like Jack.

"Besides," Billy continued, taking his towel and wiping his brow before throwing it over his shoulder. "You've been training here with me for almost a year and you've already surpassed me. Tell me that's not supernatural."

I shrugged sheepishly. "I'm a fast learner. What can I say?"

So, I hadn't exactly been sitting on my ass taking phone calls and filing case files for the last year. While I couldn't exactly go running after the hunters on my own—I didn't even know where they were—what I could do was make myself less of a liability. Being a human servant had some extra benefits. Faster reflexes, heightened senses, and now thanks to Billy, a background in mixed martial arts and weapons.

"You ready to go to the back?" Billy jerked his head toward the door at the back of his studio. The front was covered in blue and black mats where we trained with a few free weights lined around the edges.

"Yeah, but only if you're not going to tease me anymore." I gave him a pointed look as I followed him into the back room. Here, Billy had five stalls lined up, pointed toward a long room with different targets spread throughout the space. We had begun with normal targets, the kind with the silhouette of a person that they used at official shooting ranges. When Billy found out that my skills were far above the norm, we'd moved on to moving targets. Not that they were much more of a challenge for me now. Before I became a vampire servant, I couldn't have been able to hit a target if it were five inches in front of me. In fact, I probably would have ended up shooting myself. Exploring my new abilities had been interesting for sure. Especially with my raging hormones needing an outlet.

I shifted before the booth, smiling to myself as I remembered all the creative ways Darren and I had relieved those hormonal fits of mine.

"So, what's on the schedule for today?" I wiggled my fingers and cracked my neck, prepping for whatever Billy threw at me.

Billy went over to the cabinet where he kept his weapons and punched in a code. Reaching inside, he gave me no warning before spinning around and throwing something at me. I jumped to the side, narrowly avoiding it.

"What the fuck, Billy?" I glared at him and then at the dagger sticking out of the opposite wall. I marched over to the wall and pulled the dagger out, waving it in the air. "You could have killed me!"

With a knowing smile, Billy pointed at me. "But I didn't."

I frowned and dropped the dagger to my side. "That's beside the point."

"You can't tell me that wasn't supernatural of some kind. No one has that kind of reflexes without years of training." Billy shook his head in disbelief. "I'm an ex-marine, believe me. Even some of the guys don't have that kind of intuition. I don't know why you even came to me in the first place."

"I told you," I repressed a frustrated growl, "I'm trying to be prepared for—"

"That ex-boyfriend of yours, right." Billy's tone sounded like he didn't quite believe the lie I'd been telling him over the last few months. Turning back to the cabinet, he pulled out another few daggers and brought them over to me. "Since we have gone through all the gun exercises I have and you've aced them," he gave me a pointed look which I avoided, fiddling with the handle of the dagger, "I figured you should learn some other techniques. You won't always have a gun around to protect you. And you need to be able to fight with other weapons."

"And you thought daggers," I lifted up the dagger in my hand with a raised brow, "were the answer? Aren't they a little..." I huffed. "When am I ever going to have a dagger lying around? A steak knife, yes, but a dagger?" I moved to cross my arms, but then remembered the dagger and dropped my arms again.

Billy moved into position in front of the targets and tossed three daggers in rapid succession. Turning back to me with a straight face, Billy pointed a dagger at me. "Because while I don't quite believe all this ex-boyfriend stuff," I opened my mouth to argue, but he stopped me, "it's your business and I don't want to pry. However, I do know that someone like you, someone who just eleven months ago came in here looking like she'd never thrown a punch in her life, is gearing up for something. Something big, and far be it from me to keep you from being fully prepared for whatever you are getting yourself into." He held the handle of the dagger out to me. "So, you're up."

I pressed my lips into a grateful smile, taking the hilt. "Thanks. You don't know how much I appreciate all this."

"Just stay alive and that's thanks enough."

I took Billy's place in front of the targets and threw the dagger. It hit the target just shy of the center. I twisted to Billy and cocked a brow. "I don't think that'll be a problem."

Several hours and even more sweat later, I left Billy's to head back home. I hated to lie to Billy, but I couldn't very well tell him the truth. Not like he would believe me anyway.

I hardly believed it. Though, all this prepping to fight the hunters didn't do me any good if I couldn't find them. They weren't exactly listed anywhere. They only revealed themselves to vampires and other hunters. Which, while I wasn't prepared to be the former, I hoped to convince them I was the latter. I just needed a starting point.

"Darren!" I tossed my keys and purse onto the side table and walked farther into the house. A delicious smell filled the air. I followed it to the kitchen where I found Darren at the island and a familiar, grey-haired head at the stove. "Gretchen! When did you get here?"

The plump older woman turned from the stove and greeted me with a warm smile. "Piper. Look at you. You've changed so much." Releasing the handle of the spoon in the pot she had been stirring, Gretchen hurried over to me, pulling me into a tight embrace.

I hugged her back tightly, enjoying the comfort of an old friend. "I'm so happy to see you, Gretchen." I glanced over her shoulder to meet Darren's gaze. arching a brow at him. He simply offered me a mysterious smile before popping a slice of cucumber into his mouth from the tray on the table.

Gretchen released me to go back to her pot, which had begun to boil. She picked up the wooden spoon once more and turned down the heat. "I'm so glad to see you and Darren have grown so close. I was worried for you two, out here all alone without the masters." She gave us a knowing look before winking.

I flushed and slid onto the stool next to Darren. He placed his hand on top of mine, bringing it to his mouth to press a kiss to the top of it. What happened between Darren and me hadn't been planned. It'd just happened. One night, I was freaking out about being left here and determined to hunt down the others with or without his help, and then next thing I knew Darren and I were kissing. It kind of spiraled out from there.

"So..." I reached out to the vegetable tray and snatched a carrot stick off of it, dipping it into the bowl of ranch beside it. I slid the carrot into my mouth sucking off the ranch. Darren grunted beside me, his eyes fixated on my lips. With a suppressed grin, I chomped down on the carrot. Turning back to Gretchen, I asked, "Not that I'm not happy to see you, but what made you come all the way out here?"

Offering me a far sassier than normal smirk, Gretchen turned the stove off before wiping her hands on her apron. "Do I need a reason to come visit my two favorite people in the world?"

I exchanged a look with Darren. "Of course not. Just we're not the safest people to be around right now. Shouldn't you be keeping a low profile?"

"Pfft." Gretchen waved me off as she sat out three bowls. "I'm old enough to know when I should be hiding and when I should be helping." She gave me a pointed look, then began to fill the bowls with what she'd been mixing in her pot.

My nose had me focusing more on what Gretchen was serving than what she was saying. It was some kind of goulash, and my stomach agreed it was far more important than her impromptu visit. A little more greedily than I should have, I took the bowl from her before she could even finish pushing it toward me. Dipping my spoon into the bowl, I wasted no time popping it into my mouth.

Big mistake.

"Ho...hot!" I swallowed painfully, my eyes watering as I waved a hand in front of my mouth. Gretchen pushed a glass of water to me with a shake of her head.

"See what happens when you get ahead of yourself?" Gretchen gave me a chastising look before handing Darren his bowl and taking her own to the last seat at the island next to me. "Which is one of the reasons I have come. I know you're trying to find a way to help the masters, and I don't want to overstep my bounds, but are you sure you want to get involved?"

My brows shot up and I turned in my seat to face her. "What? Of course I do. I'm not just going to wait around here for them to do something. We've been stuck here for a year now, and what has that gotten us? Nothing."

"Nothing?" Darren asked, a bit of hurt to his tone.

I twisted quickly back to the man at my side, grabbing his arm before he could close down. "That's not what I meant and you know it." I sighed heavily, holding his arm with both hands. "You know I love being here with you, but you have to admit this wasn't supposed to be a permanent situation. We won't age, Darren! We'll stay the same as long as Antoine is alive and that could be two thousand years from now or two seconds. I don't know about you, but I'd rather have a more definite future than that." I took a breath and closed my eyes for a second. When I opened them again, I was staring into Darren's dark orbs. "I love you and want to be with you, but I love the others too. I can't just leave them to their fate. Especially when it's tied so closely to ours."

Darren inclined his head slowly, cupping my face with one hand. "I know. We will get them back. Won't we, Gretchen?"

A soft hand rubbed my back and I shifted toward the older woman.

"Don't worry, dear, I'm not just here to feed you." Gretchen smiled sadly. "I have some news."

"News?" Now that had my full attention. "What kind of news?"

Gretchen stood and walked across the room. She picked up her purse and pulled out her phone, bringing it back over to us. "While you've been hiding out here and with the masters on the run, I've been watching the house. Checking the mail, looking for break ins, the like. Nothing has been stolen, thankfully, but there have been a few suspicious characters lurking about." She brought up a video on her phone, which I recognized from one of the security cameras. There were three figures dressed in black with far more firepower than they should have for solicitors, especially in the middle of the day. "Three times I have caught them on camera. They haven't broken into the house yet, but this last time I went to check the mail, one of them showed up."

I gasped, clutching her arm. "Are you okay? They didn't hurt you, did they?"

"No, no." Gretchen patted my hand, setting her phone down. "They didn't hurt me. Though, they did want to know where my employers were." Her eyes grew hard at that statement.

"What'd you tell them?"

"Nothing, of course." She leaned back, her brows raised. "What kind of person do you take me for? I'm not going to tell the bad guys where my family is. Even though they offered me tons of money to do so."

I frowned, pursing my lips before asking, "Why wouldn't they hurt you for it when you said no?"

Darren spoke then. "Because it's against their code. They don't hurt humans. At least, not the non-human servant kind."

"So, they'd hurt you or me to get to them though," I pointed out, my stomach rolling with anxiety and growing anger.

"Yes. Which is why we must stop them at all costs."

Darren's words surprised me. I looked between Darren and Gretchen, my brows furrowed. "I thought you were against me going after them. It's too dangerous for such a breakable woman such as me," I mocked, repeating his words to me several months ago.

"But you're not so breakable anymore, are you?" Darren scanned over my form, his fingers trailing across the muscles I'd gained over my time working with Billy. "Nor are you unable to protect yourself. In fact, you may be more formidable than even me."

I snorted. "Yeah, okay. That's all good and well, but it doesn't help us find the hunters, and without them we're pretty much stuck here."

"Except," Gretchen pulled my attention back, "I know where they are."

My brows rose. "How's that?"

With a sly grin, Gretchen pulled up an app on her phone, showing a blinking red dot on a map of Atlanta. "You didn't think I was just hired for my cooking, did you? I slipped a tracker onto one of those hunters while they were contemplating what to do with an old woman. And now..." The red dot moved across the screen and then stopped on a large estate.

"We know where they are," I finished for her. Plans formed in my mind, and all of sudden my time in Seabrick seemed to be short-lived. Soon, my life might be back to normal. Or as normal as it could get.

Chapter 4

Antoine

A YEAR IN THE span of a vampire wasn't very long at all. A blink of time in the long, infinity of forever. However, this last year had been like no other. Every moment away from Darren and Piper felt like knives digging into my veins.

Even hundreds of miles away, I could feel everything they felt. Every quiver of fear. Every burst of joy. Then there was the never-ending black hole of rage, which at any moment would fill to the brim, and who knew what would come from it when that happened.

Unsurprisingly, the anger came from Piper. Darren always had been more in control of his emotions than her. He'd been with me far longer, so I supposed he has had more practice.

Still, it was worrisome. My brothers and I had been on the move almost constantly since the hunters caught our scent back at Boris's manor. From Frankfurt to London and then finally back to the U.S. where I could keep a better eye on Darren and Piper. Not that it had done much good.

We were only ever able to get away for a day or two every month and never more than one of us at a time. The hunters were more tenacious than I had expected. Then again, with one of the most powerful master vampires terminated, they didn't have much else to do. Chasing us must be one of the only things giving the suped-up humans a purpose.

"You're an idiot if you think that." Rayne snorted, plopping down on the ratty couch, which at one point used to be red but was now more of an ugly brown.

"Do my ears deceive me, or am I still the head of this household?" I narrowed my gaze on Rayne. His shaggy red hair had been cut short with only the top part slightly longer. The long-sleeved, ribbed black shirt he wore had several holes in it, but not as many as the dark jeans on his legs. The combat boots he'd acquired from somewhere along with the rest of his outfit were covered in mud.

We'd all had to make sacrifices for the sake of our family, the disgusting motel we were staying in for one, but Rayne had chosen to change himself far more drastically than the others.

"Not you though," Rayne argued, interrupting my thoughts once more with a sneer. "And as I see it. You're not head of anything anymore. None of us are. We're just another group of bloodsuckers the hunters can pick off one by one."

"Wallowing in self-pity has never been a good look for you, Rayne. Best not to start now." I sighed and lifted my phone to check my messages. Nothing from Wynn yet.

I'd sent him to check on Piper a week ago and he still hadn't checked in. I had begun to think something had happened.

"Wynn's fine." Rayne shifted on the couch, glaring at the pale peeling yellow wallpaper around us. "He messaged a few hours ago that he was going to make a stop."

My hand tightened around my phone as I held back my need to lash out. "Why wasn't I informed?"

"Well, oh stick up your ass one, if you weren't in here moping, then you would have been with me when I found out." Rayne slid his fingers through the front of his hair, fluffing it up. "I was getting dinner with the twins."

Crossing one leg over the other, I glared at the door of the motel room. "You shouldn't be going out in such a big group. I've told you this time and time again." My voice rose, unable to keep myself in check any longer. "Pairs are all we can risk and only at scheduled times. Your turn wasn't until four with Marcus."

Rayne stood from the couch abruptly. "Well, tell that to your pet, because Marcus has been gone all day. I wasn't going to risk not getting to eat tonight. It's already been three days."

My own hunger ate at my stomach and my fangs ached to sink into someone. It could be that my need for blood has caused me to lose control of myself, but at that moment all I wanted to do was rip Rayne's throat out for daring to speak back to me.

Rayne backed away slowly, his hands up in front of him. "You could do with a bite too.

Especially before you hear what Wynn has to say."

Flashing my fangs at him, I bolted to my feet. My hand raced out too fast for the human eye, but not for Rayne's. He quickly dodged my hand and jumped back to the door, his hand going to the doorknob.

I took a step toward him but then stopped myself. Taking a moment, I closed my eyes and worked on calming myself. I couldn't lose it now and hurt one of my own. No matter how much he frustrated me to no end. After I felt I wasn't in danger of lashing out again, I opened my eyes and focused on Rayne.

"My apologies. It seems I, too, need to feed." I adjusted the cuffs of my suit jacket and brushed my long pale strands over my shoulder. "As for the matter of Marcus, he's on recon for nearby hunters. He should be back soon. What of Wynn?"

Rayne turned the doorknob and threw the door open, revealing our disheveled, dark-haired brother. "He's here."

Scanning over Wynn's form and finding no injury or other reason for his delay, I prepared to lay it into him, only for the vampire to lift a dark blue ice chest. "Hungry? I brought dinner."

Rayne sighed, his shoulders sagging. "Thank God. Our lord and master here was two seconds away from tearing my head off."

Wynn's lips quirked up. "It's a good thing I stopped by a blood bank on the way home then, brother."

I narrowed my eyes on him and took my seat on the couch once more. "It was a rash and unnecessary risk."

Rayne snorted.

"It was necessary, *mon cher*." Wynn threw a packet of blood at me.

I caught it midair and lowered it to my mouth. Tearing into the side of the pack, I grumbled, "Don't call me that."

The moment the blood touched my tongue, I couldn't hold back a groan of pleasure. The others moved into the room, keeping their distance from me as I drained another bag of blood. When I opened my eyes, four out of five of my brothers stood before me. The twins had on matching grey hoodies, stating they went to the local college, along with gym shorts. We tried to integrate ourselves into each place we hid out in so we didn't stand out. The town we were in now was a college town, which made it easy pickings for feeding, but harder for those of us who looked more than the average college age. Which was why I'd sent

Wynn to see Piper while I kept to our motel room.

"Better?" Drake quirked a brow.

"Much." I tossed the bag aside and placed a hand on my knee. "How did it go?"

"Well, Allister got himself surrounded by a horde of sorority girls and we had to push a bit of power to get out of there without getting mobbed or stripped on the spot." Drake chuckled, nudging his brother in the arm. Allister's lips ticked up slightly at his twin's words, but didn't comment further.

"While that sounds entertaining, I was referring to Wynn." I shifted my gaze from the twins to Wynn. He lounged on the dingy, vomit green bedspread with a look of utter disdain on his face. No doubt in reference to the pitiful lodging we had found ourselves in.

"Speaking of interesting," Wynn murmured, with a sly quirk of his lips that didn't promise anything I would like. "Things with Piper and Darren are going well."

"Are you sure?" I arched a brow. "I feel far more anger than I should be if everything is going well."

Wynn threw his head back and laughed. The others gave him a curious look, but I simply waited for him to elaborate. "Oh, yes. Piper is truly and surely, as they say, pissed off. I barely made it out of there with my head on my shoulders. We must find a better way of checking in on them than just once a month. I fear she won't stay in one place for too much longer. It's already been far too long." He seemed like he had more to say, but he didn't elaborate further.

"Yes," I mused, lifted a hand to my face. "I wish we had better news, but unfortunately, with no way to find the hunters, we are simply stuck on the defense. Marcus is out now doing recon."

"Recon?" Wynn sat forward, his hands laced between his legs. "What could he possibly hope to learn?"

My mouth tugged up at the edges. "With any luck, where the hunters take refuge. Marcus will let a hunter find him and then follow them back to their lair."

"Lair?" Drake chuckled.

"For lack of a better word." I glowered at him, then I turned my attention back to Wynn. "Anything else to report?"

Wynn's face takes on a curious expression I couldn't describe, but Rayne thankfully figured it out for me.

Rayne jumped back from the others with a look of shock and horror on his face. "Piper and Darren are what?"

Wynn offered Rayne a lazy grin, lifting a hand to wiggle his little finger into his ear.

"Shout a little louder, little brother. I don't think the hunters in town heard you."

The twins carried identical expressions of confusion and interest, while I waited patiently for Rayne or Wynn to explain.

"How could this have happened?" Rayne continued, jerking his arms around him. His agitation showing with each movement. "I thought they tolerated each other." Then, without warning, Rayne spun on me, pointing a finger in my face. "This is your fault. If you hadn't opened that can of worms, my Piper wouldn't be lowering herself to...to playing house with that stick in the mud." Rayne's face turned as red as his hair as he twisted back around to the others. "And I blame all of us for leaving her alone with him for so long."

Drake grabbed Rayne by the shoulders and stopped him from going back and forth like a spin top. "Would you chill out already and just tell us what's going on?"

Wynn interrupted Rayne before he could get another word out. "It seems our dear Darren has far more charm than we believed. He's somehow wormed his way not only into Piper's bed, but her heart as well."

While the others stiffened at Wynn's words, I hummed. On the outside, I seemed calm and collected, but on the inside, I boiled with jealousy and rage. Not because I hated the fact that Piper and Darren were together, but because I hadn't been there to watch it develop. Two of the people I cared for most in this world had found solace in each other. If that wasn't ironic, I didn't know what was.

My brothers argued and debated how the serious Darren had been able to woo the hyperactive klutz that was Piper, while I closed my eyes and focused. My mind shifted from my body and flew through the air. My conscience sped through the emptiness until it came into the nearest crow in Seabrick.

Lifting my wings, I took to the air. The salty breeze from the ocean filled my senses as I swooped and flapped in the sky. I shifted through the trees and passed the houses, barely noticing the humans wandering the streets around me. Finally, I lowered myself onto the nearby branch of a small house near the beach.

Peering through the window of the living room, I searched for a familiar face. Neither Piper nor Darren were in the living room. I strained my ears toward the sounds coming from farther in the house. Giggling and groans. Taking flight once more, I glided through the air until I rounded the house, landing on the windowsill to the bedroom.

The room was simple, but it had touches of Piper and Darren in it. The bathroom door was open, spilling light into the otherwise dark room. Clothes were strewn over a nearby chair, a bra had been carelessly dropped on the floor, and there was a stack of romance novels on the side table. Nothing of Darren's was thrown about the room, but there was a small pile of his clothes on the dresser and a pair of white gloves on the nightstand.

Another giggle pulled my attention back to the bathroom door. The water from the showerhead tinged against the tile, disrupted by what I assumed were bodies in the way. I waited for the water to cut off and then feet padded out of the shower, barely audible. Then there was giggling again.

"If you get me dirty, I'll have to take a shower all over again." Piper's voice came out husky and muffled as if something covered her mouth.

"Then I shall have to clean you, thoroughly." I recognized the sound of desire in Darren's voice as they stumbled out of the bathroom, nude and still slick with water. I waited for Darren to insist on cleaning up the water they were dripping all over the wooden floor. He didn't. Darren's hands slid down to cup Piper's ass, dragging her closer to him as they collapsed on the bed. To my utter surprise, Darren smiled. An open and honest grin that spread from one ear to the other. I'd never seen such a thing on Darren's face in all our time together.

Giving them their privacy, I withdrew from the crow. My mind flew through the air between Georgia and Rhode Island, settling back into my body.

My brothers were no longer arguing, their voices low as they discussed the movements of the hunters nearby. Wynn noticed my movements first, pausing mid-sentence to look to me. The others followed suit.

"Well?" Allister asked with a hint of apprehension in his voice.

I uncrossed my legs and brushed my pants off as I stood. "What? Are you afraid of a little competition? Do you think that Piper does not have room in her heart for each of us?" All but Wynn shifted. He seemed unaffected by my human servants' coupling, unlike the others. "There is nothing to fear. Be happy they are finding enjoyment in each other rather than outside of the family. God only knows what Piper could get herself into if she wasn't thoroughly distracted."

Wynn snorted. "Isn't that the truth."

Chapter 5

Marcus

HUNTING THE VAMPIRE HUNTERS was not quite as exciting as it sounded. Hours of waiting around and nothing to show for it. I even left a trail of bitten humans to lead them to me, but as of yet I have not gained the attention of a single hunter.

When Antoine and I had concocted this plan, I'd been against it. I thought we should have called in the favors owed to us by the other vampire masters to find the hunters, but Antoine didn't want to put our fates in the hands of others. Something I couldn't disagree with. We'd already been screwed over by more than our fair share of master vampires. Luck hadn't been on our side as of late, and I'd much rather we took things into our own hands.

Hence the plan.

The vampire hunters had to be close. We'd been in Rhode Island longer than usual, so we could execute this plan. Not that our brothers knew about it. If they did, they would have objected for sure. The hunters usually found us within a few weeks of wherever we hid out. It's been a month. They should be here by now.

A light drizzle came down around me from where I stood. The awning of a drugstore that had long since closed hung above me, shielding me from the rain. The water didn't bother me, but the rain would wash away my scent, something I didn't want to do. I needed the hunters to find me for our plan to work.

It was a foolish plan. One of desperation. My brothers and I were tired of running. Tired of always looking over our shoulders. We wanted to go home. And I knew they wanted to see Piper again.

I, too, missed the pretty human who had captured the hearts of my brothers. I'd only been to visit her twice over the last year, and both times it was as if I could finally breathe again. Not that I needed breath to live. All I knew was she made everything right. Something I hadn't felt in a long time. My mind drifted to the last time I had felt any semblance of peace. A time when everything in my life made sense and I had a purpose.

"You're a long way from home, knight," a gravelly voice announced, stepping out from the shadows of a nearby tree. "It isn't safe here for people like you."

I glared down at the man, who had yet to reveal his face beneath his hood. "People like me?"

He gestured a hand in my direction. It was spotted and wizened and long nails tipped each finger. "Knights of the Catholic Church should not venture out this far by themselves. Especially, at night." The man coughed a laugh, his hand going up to his face beneath the hood.

The sky above had turned dark over my hours of traveling across the desert on horseback. Exhaustion ate at me as well as my horse. Unfortunately, there was no place to take shelter. I supposed I would be sleeping beneath the stars tonight.

"Thank you for your concern, but I will be alright." I glanced back to the hooded figure. "The Muslim troops have gone east. I plan to be well away from here before they can find me." I paused and looked back down to the figure. "You should be on your way as well if you value your life. This is not a time to be venturing out on your own without an escort. You'll be lucky to be killed on sight and not be taken to be tortured for whichever side you sit on."

The hooded figure laughed. "Oh, I do not belong to anyone's side but my own." He stepped closer to my horse, making it neigh and shift nervously. I tried to reassure my mount, but the figure caught my wrist where my armor ended and my gloved hand began. "But if you are offering your services, I would gladly accept."

Before I knew what was happening, I was pulled from my horse and knocked to the ground. The figure, which I had thought to be an older man, was far quicker than expected. My ears rang as my helmet was ripped from my head. I reached for my sword and glared at the man.

"Unhand me, you beast, or I shall show you why we are called God's army." I grabbed at the cloak, trying to get a handhold on him. His hood fell back and I gasped, my eyes

going wide with horror. "A demon. You're a demon. Begone! In the name of the Father, Son, and Holy Spirit, I banish you back to your hellish plane. Leave me be."

The creature threw his head back and laughed, his ears pointed and his teeth sharpened into spikes. Red eyes bore into me right before he attacked. I didn't have a chance to swing my sword before sharp pain burrowed into my neck. Then I remembered nothing but the sounds of my screams. I screamed until my throat burned, not stopping until I could no longer keep my head up, and my eyes closed. Then there was darkness.

I shook my head of the memory. My last night as a human had been gruesome. Full of pain and blood. Boris hadn't changed me right away. He'd made me last days. Nights. It was hard to find food readily available in the desert, he'd said. He had to make me last.

Scoffing, I rubbed the back of my head and then crossed my arms. Now was not the time to be nostalgic. Boris was dead. There was nothing keeping me from moving on with my life. I could only hope that God would forgive me for the acts I'd done for an undeniable monster.

My head jerked up.

I shifted to the left, narrowly dodging an arrow aimed right for my head. Pulling my knives from their sheaths at my sides, I spun around to face my attackers. Three hunters approached me. They weren't even trying to be subtle as they walked brazenly down the middle of the street.

"There you are," I mused aloud, my lips ticking up in amusement. "I was beginning to think we'd lost you."

The middle hunter, a young woman with long, raven-colored hair and a crossbow in her hands sneered, "Were you looking for us, vampire? I'm so sorry we have kept you waiting." She cocked her crossbow and aimed it at me. "Where are the others?"

I held my daggers out at my sides and shrugged. "What others? I work alone."

The hunter to the left snickered. "As if we believe that. We scented you bloodsuckers the moment you stepped into this town. It's only a matter of time until we find you all and kill you. Give it up, and we'll make your death a quick one."

"I doubt that," I grumbled.

"Fine then, have it your way." The female lifted her crossbow, but before she could shoot me with it, I was moving.

I knew the plan was to have them chase me, but if I didn't at least try to defend myself they would be suspicious. With my daggers drawn, I ducked one way and then the other, avoiding the bolts coming my way. The woman cursed as she fumbled with the next bolt. I came up underneath her crossbow and slashed at her side. She dropped the crossbow and jumped back, but not fast enough. The tip of my dagger sliced into the side of her clothes and blood tinged the air.

"You bastard," the hunter on the left snarled, coming at me at full force. "How dare you draw blood from our dear, Mizuki. Die, bloodsucker!"

Was this guy for real? I resisted the urge to roll my eyes as I easily dodged his attacks. He swung his sword like a newborn pup. Weak and unused to carrying a sword. I smacked his wrist with the flat side of my dagger.

"Fuck!" The man dropped his sword, falling back onto his ass.

I could kill him right there, but that wasn't the plan.

Ignoring the downed man, I turned around and lifted my daggers into an X, blocking the sword coming down at me. Gritting my teeth, I allowed myself to drop to one knee, pretending that the hunter was getting the best of me.

If I were a prouder man, I'd never pretended I was the weaker opponent in the hopes of catching them off guard. When I was a knight, I surely would never have allowed my honor to be tarnished in such a manner. However, being a vampire under the cruel thumb of Boris would destroy the honor of even the most loyal and proud man.

"We've got you now, fucker," the first man crowed as the female, Mizuki, leveled the crossbow at me once more.

I guess I've played with them long enough.

I shoved the sword back easily, making the hunter fall onto the ground, his head cracking against the road. I kicked out, knocking the crossbow from Mizuki's hands before spinning on my heels. "You'll have to catch me first."

A low curse, followed by several arrows whisking through the air, chased me as I dodged and weaved. Now that I had them on my trail, I had to circle back until they grew tired and returned to their base.

I darted into an alley and jumped, grabbing the lowest rung of the metal ladder leading up to a fire escape, before I raced up the ladder's rungs, taking them two at a time. Leaping the final rung to the top, I glanced down to the ground to see if the hunters had caught up yet.

No sign of them. Frowning, I waited a moment until I heard hurried footsteps heading my way. Turning from the edge of the fire escape, I braced myself, bending my knees and pushing as much power as I could into my jump. I shot up into the sky and landed with a heavy thud on top of the brick building. The ground of the roof broke beneath me, but I didn't waste time worrying about it. The footfalls were closer now.

Pivoting around in one smooth movement, I ran toward the opposite side of the roof. The edge came into view and at the last moment, I jumped. Thankfully, the roof of the building next to me was lower, allowing me to land in a roll. I came up instantly and kept moving. If I knew the hunters, they would have figured out that I'd gone up and would be coming after me any moment. Slower, but I still couldn't tarry.

Once I was sure I'd put enough distance between us, I dropped from the side of the building, landing heavily on the sidewalk. My legs held and I made it two more steps before something small and sharp hit me in the side of the neck.

My hand went to it, my mind clouding as I pulled the small item from my flesh. A dart. Laced with poison no doubt by the way my skin was going numb. I found my vision darkening and I dropped to my knees.

"Not so slow now, are we, vampire." The voice of the woman, Mizuki, filled my ears. "Now we'll get answers from you, one way or another."

I grunted as I collapsed to the ground, my face hitting the pavement with a smack.

"Quickly, the poison won't keep him out long," Mizuki commanded, and footsteps hurried to my side. "We have to get him back to base. The commander will want to interrogate him personally."

"But is that wise, Mizuki? What if the others follow us?" a voice I didn't recognize asked, but my mind was going blank and I couldn't listen in any longer.

Well, on the bright side, I was finally going to see where their base of operations was located. Unfortunately, Antoine was not going to be pleased.

Chapter 6

Piper

"ARE YOU SURE YOU want to do this?" Darren inquired, as he worked on unpacking his suitcase into the hotel dresser drawer. Seriously, who even used those?

While I couldn't see his face, I could hear the apprehension in his voice. Neither of us thought this was a safe idea, but it was the only one I had.

"You know, you can back out now. We can go back to Seabrick and no one would be the wiser." He finished putting his things away and closed the drawer, turning around to face me.

I sat on the edge of the queen-sized bed in the beige hotel room. Literally, everything was beige. The carpet, the walls, even the bedspread. The only other color in the room were the dressers, and those were only a darker shade of beige. Just sitting in the room was making me feel depressed.

"I don't see what other option we have." I shifted on the mattress, not used to the outfit I wore. If I was going to play vampire hunter, I had to look the part. That included dressing in all black. Logical I guess for nighttime raids, but really, who was the person that had a color phobia? 'Cause this outfit, while slimming, could use a dash of color. At least, some varying shades. Burgundy wouldn't be so bad. It was dark, and if you bled no one would notice. Or maybe brown. No, not brown. Too many poop jokes. Still, I could have done without the leather pants riding up my ass. I couldn't even wear underwear with these things. Alas, there weren't many options I could choose from for a vampire hunter persona. I couldn't exactly go to Hunters 'R Us for my outfit. And from what

Rayne told me about the hunters in Club Dead, this was the kind of stuff they wore. Bondage with a side of badass. I guess I could live with it. At least until I got them off my guys' tails.

I sighed. The things we did for love.

Standing, I checked the different straps I had attached to the pants for my daggers. While I had joked around with Billy about never needing to use them, I made sure I had some just in case. I didn't know exactly what kind of gear the hunters would be toting, and I wanted to be prepared. I already had a crossbow to strap to my back and a gun. Billy had given me a shoulder holster as a gift when I told him I was heading out of town.

"Not that it's my business, but better to be safe than get a hole in the foot." We'd shared a laugh over that before I hugged him tightly. He didn't ask, but hugged me back before wishing me luck. That guy might not know everything there was to know about me, but I could trust him to have my back. I was sure if I had asked him, he would have come with me, but I couldn't bring him into this. This was my fight. Mine and the Durands'.

"I'll check in every day at the drop point," I reminded Darren with a lifted brow. "Fifth and Memorial? The trashcan on the corner?"

Darren placed his hands on my shoulders and rubbed them up and down. "Yes, I'll be waiting with bated breath."

I smiled softly up at him, a small chuckle coming out before I shoved it down. If I laughed, I might cry, and I couldn't handle that right now. Not to mention it would ruin my mascara.

So, instead, I let Darren hold me for a moment before pushing away. I knew if I stayed any longer, I wouldn't be able to make myself do what needed to be done. I loved the guys, but sometimes it took a woman to get the job finished, and I was just the one to do it.

"Do you want me to come with you?" Darren offered, not for the first time. "I could pose as a hunter as well."

I shook my head, my ponytail whipping me in the neck with the movement. "No, it'll be easier to blend in with one rather than two unfamiliar hunters. Besides, they know about the two of us. It would look suspicious." I took a deep breath and let it out, my eyes staring down at nothing. "No, I have to do it alone. Besides," I gave him a salacious grin, "a pretty hunter who's lost her way is far more likely to get information than if I were attached."

Darren's brows furrowed and his lips pressed into a tight line.

I reached up and brushed my finger between his brows. "Don't give me that look. I have far more than enough dick in my life. I don't need to add any more."

"I'm not worried about that." Darren frowned harder.

"Then what is it?"

Darren let out a long breath and shook his head. "I'm afraid you'll make rash decisions in there by yourself. You don't exactly have the best track record."

I gaped at him. "I do not! I mean, ugh, I do too!" Darren quirked a brow. "Fine. Name one. No, three instances."

Lifting his hand, Darren put down one finger. "Getting employed by a house of vampires."

I scoffed, "How the hell was I supposed to know that? That's the agency's fault, not mine."

"Drawing Valentine's attention when you were clearly instructed to keep a low profile." He lowered another finger.

"He was deranged," I countered, and then added, "And if it were anyone's fault it was the others for being overprotective." I crossed my arms and nodded. "Valentine would never have had any interest in me had the others not thrown their dicks everywhere."

Darren inclined his head. "I will concede that one. However, there was the time you ran off on your own in Boris's home. Being mouthy at the introductions. Taking the payment for the information from Morpheus." I opened my mouth to argue, but Darren kept going. "Getting a job with an attractive boss." I clipped my mouth shut and glared, making Darren smirk. "As well as getting involved with any of us in the first place. Admit it. You attract trouble."

I opened and shut my mouth before placing my hands on my hips and turning my head away. "Fine. I can see your point. But still, I can handle this. I won't do anything stupid. Cross my heart." I did the gesture across my chest as well.

Darren took my hand in his, bringing it to his mouth for a kiss. "I have no doubt you will try. Good luck, Piper."

My gaze softened on Darren before he released my hand. I nodded my head once and headed for the door. It was time. I couldn't hold off any longer.

Leaving the hotel, I walked down the street. I couldn't take my car because they might check my tags for my identity. In fact,

I'd left everything that could trace me back to the Durands at the house in Seabrick. Darren had booked the hotel room under an alias and paid cash. No one but us and Gretchen knew we were here.

I'd taken some sick days at the office to carry out this plan. So, as far as Jack and Bethany were aware, I was out with the flu. I just hoped I would be done before I ran out of time off. Not that losing that job would hurt me or anything. The Durands were still paying my salary and besides, this was all for them anyway.

The black boots I wore clomped against the concrete, my leather pants tucked into the tops at the calf. The shoulder holster sat on top of my long-sleeved shirt, the V-neck of it showing off a generous amount of cleavage. I hadn't been kidding when I said I hoped a lone, attractive female would draw the right kind of attention. The kind that led to information and a way to get my guys off the radar and my life back in order. I didn't know about the rest of them, but I had about enough vampire drama to last me a lifetime.

The vampire hunters' base of operations sat on an acre of land surrounded by a sharp-edged fence. The mansion behind the offensive gate looked more like an old museum than a base for vampire hunters.

Without a sign showing it was one thing or the other, it just seemed like an unassuming, stuffy old building. One that I had to somehow get inside of.

Walking around the fence, I found the front of the gate. It had a call box with a keypad to type in some code.

Damn. I should have thought of that.

What was I going to do now?

I glanced up at the gate and the menacing sharp points. I winced. No way was I going to be able to get over that.

Blowing a raspberry, I clicked my tongue and shifted from side to side. I guess I should just go back to the hotel room. What a waste of a good outfit. Plus all the time and energy it took to get it on and the teary goodbye to Darren. I didn't know if I had it in me to do that again.

Just as I was about to turn away from the gate, a crackling voice came over the speaker. "Did you forget the passcode again?"

I scratched the side of my face and bent down to the box, trying to look sheepish. "Uh, yeah. Sorry. Do you think you could let me in?"

"Fine," the voice snapped. "Just write it down next time."

"Of course!" I straightened up, lifting my hand to my forehead in a salute. I didn't know why I was doing it, or if they could even see me, but it felt like the right thing to do. Seconds later, there was a buzz and the gate popped open on its own.

Well, that was lucky.

Or it was a trap.

Nope. Nope. This was a good thing. I couldn't be in deep shit yet. I might have had bad luck, but not that bad. I thought. Maybe. Whatever. I wasn't looking a gift hunter in the mouth.

Sauntering through the gate, I walked with as much confidence as I could. If I was a vampire hunter, I had to ooze badassery. I'd never heard of a wimpy and simpering vampire hunter. And I doubted they would believe my disguise if I acted that way.

The closer I got to the entrance of the building, the less confident I felt. The shadows seemed darker than normal, every sound made me jump in place. What was wrong with me? I shook my head and forced my back straight and my eyes forward. The guys were depending on me. I had to do this. There was no other way to get the hunters off their trail.

Once at the door, I didn't hesitate to open it. Now was not the time to be indecisive. The hunters would be able to smell the weakness on me and then this would be all for nothing.

Inside the manor, hunters sprawled out on various couches and chairs. Its entryway was a lot larger than the House of Durand, with stairs going up one side of the wall. They didn't bother with decorations or even with matching furniture. Everything seemed to be for functional purposes only. Including that large rack of weapons that lined the back wall.

Holy mother of all that was badass. Billy would have a field day with this! They had every weapon I could imagine, and then some I never dreamed of. My eyes I drifted over the weapons before stopping on a ball with sharp-pointed spikes. Yowch. That looked painful.

"Hey, you!"

I jolted in place. My gaze darted from the weapon rack to the hunter coming right for me. A few of the other hunters looked up from where they were repairing their weapons or talking in low voices, but the majority of them didn't even give me a second glance, or a first one, for that matter. Not like the beefy one who didn't halt his trajectory until he stopped right in front of me.

If anyone in this place did steroids, it had to be this guy. Bulging muscles strained against his sleeveless black tank top. Veins popped underneath his skin, making him look more monster than hunter. His dark eyes narrowed on me, locking me in place.

"What do you want?" I demanded with as much attitude as possible. Couldn't let them think they could walk all over me, now could I? Crossing my arms, I cocked one hip to the side and stared the man down.

Strangely enough, the man balked at my rudeness. He stopped and held his hands up. "I was just going to tell you the pin code so you wouldn't forget again."

Okay...so apparently looks could be deceiving, even in a vampire hunter lair.

He held a piece of paper out to me with a nervous look. "Uh, here."

I reached out to take it, confusion on my face. "Thanks. I guess." Were these guys really the big, bad vampire hunters making my guys run for their lives? It was hard to believe it.

The beefy guy stayed around for a moment longer, seeming to want to ask me something.

"Was there something else?" I tucked the paper into the pocket of my pants.

The big man jerked away at my words and then scratched the back of his head sheepishly. "Oh, um, you're new around here, aren't you? Are you from the main headquarters? I'm Tristan, by the way."

Headquarters. So that's what they called their base of operations. Better than calling it a lair, I supposed, but still kind of pretentious.

Quick on my feet, I shook my head. "Piper. And no, I just came back from a job in Europe. Hunting down some nest of vampires. I heard they came back to the states."

Buzzed head's expression lighted up. "Oh! You mean the Durands." He chuckled and grinned menacingly. "Those bloodsuckers keep giving everyone the slip, but I hear they got them pinned down in a college town in Rhode Island."

"Really?" I arched a brow. Was it bad that I was getting more information about my guys from the hunters than from them? I'd have to do something about that. "Then perhaps I should head that way."

"Oh, no." He grabbed my arm as I turned away. I glanced down at his hand and he dropped it immediately. "Oops, sorry. I mean, don't bother. They'll be on the move again."

I frowned. "What's that?"

"Yeah." He nodded knowingly. "You just got here, so you probably haven't had a chance to check-in, but they caught one of them and are bringing him here."

My heart dropped to my stomach. I was going to be sick. They caught one of the guys? How could it be? Wynn didn't mention anything about it when he came by.

"Oh, yeah, it just happened," Tristan continued, as if I weren't having a total meltdown. "Normally, they'd take him to the main headquarters, but since the president is visiting us right now, he ordered them to bring him here."

"They're bringing him here?" I grabbed the front of Tristan's tank top and clenched it in my fist. "Where? When?"

Tristan balked. "Uh, um, I don't know. They just gave word they were coming today."

I sighed and released him. "Oh."

"You must really have it out for those vamps to get so worked up like that." Tristan gave me a nervous smile. I nodded to put him at ease. "Well, won't be until tomorrow, if anything. Why don't you relax? I can show you around if you want? Do you have a room assigned yet?"

I let Tristan lead me farther into the manor, barely listening to anything he was saying. My mind was full of thoughts of who they could have captured. Was it Wynn? He hadn't gotten taken on the way back, had he? I didn't know, but waiting until tomorrow to find out was going to be torture.

Chapter 7

Rayne

"I DON'T LIKE THIS," Drake grumbled next to me on the airplane. "We should be looking for Marcus, not going back to Georgia."

This is a waste of time.

Swiveling in his chair, Wynn leaned on one elbow and stared lazily at Drake. "If they found Marcus, they might have found Piper and Darren as well."

"No way." Drake brushed him off with a shake of his head. "One has nothing to do with the other. Marcus was being rash." *A dumb ass plan anyway.* "It was his own fault for getting caught. It has nothing to do with Piper or Darren."

Wynn cocked a brow. "Do you really wish to chance it?"

Fucking know it all.

Drake grunted. "I guess not." His fingers clenched into fists and he pounded one onto the arm of the chair. "I'm just so tired of running. I want to go home."

"Don't you think we all do?" Allister scowled at his brother. "We're not running for the fun of it." Allister jumped out of his seat and waved a finger at Drake. "Stop thinking of yourself for five fucking seconds and think of what Marcus must be going through. They're probably torturing him as we speak, and all you can do is whine about wanting to go home! Sometimes, I don't know how I'm even related to you."

Drake sank lower into his seat, his eyes dropping down.

It wasn't often Allister yelled at his brother. In fact, it's only happened twice in the time I'd known them. For Allister to go off on him now showed how dire the situation was.

"Come now, Allister." Antoine glanced away from the window, his voice tired and strained. "We are all worried about Marcus, but there's no need to take it out on each other." Though, he was right. This was all my fault.

"No, there isn't," I interrupted him, speaking for the first time since we'd gotten on the plane. "Marcus knew what he was doing. He is the most capable of all of us. And while I can't read his thoughts, I know that right now, he would be thinking at least he learned where their base was." I offered him a reassuring smile. The atmosphere of the plane lifted a little bit, but it was still hard to be positive when one of our own was held captive or worse, dead.

Good thing they couldn't read my thoughts.

"Rayne is right. We can't do anything until we know where the base is," Allister explained, nodding in my direction. "Checking on the others is a good plan and we might also find out something useful."

Drake sighed and placed his face in his hand. "Fine. I guess I'm outvoted either way." *We're just gonna get bitched at by Piper for letting Marcus get captured anyway,* he thought

I winced. That wasn't completely untrue. Piper and Marcus might not be together yet, but she would still rip them a new one for letting even one of our members be captured. I didn't look forward to that conversation.

However, it would be worth it to have her in my arms again. It felt like a lifetime since I'd kissed her. Since I'd lain beside her and just held her as she slept. Even cleaning up one of our messes would do. God, I would give anything to see her bent over cleaning the toilet again.

"Gentlemen, we are starting our final descent." The pilot's voice came over a large speaker, interrupting my thoughts.

We buckled our seat belts and prepared for landing. Normally, we wouldn't care about wearing them. It's not like we could die from it, but we didn't have time to nurse any wounds today. We had to get to where Piper and Darren had been living and find out if they knew anything, or worse, if the hunters had found them too.

I shuddered at the thought. Just the possibility that the hunters could have my girl in their lair was more than I could take. They could be doing all manner of things to her right now and she would have no one there to save her.

We filed out of the airplane in solemn silence, each of us focused on our thoughts on what was ahead. I pulled my powers into myself, unable to bear the others' doubts and fears along with my own. Mine were bad enough.

Antoine turned to us once we sat inside of the limo. "When we arrive, refrain from telling Piper about Marcus right away. We don't need her to be hysterical before we can find out anything useful from her."

Drake snorted. "That's an understatement."

Giving Drake a sharp look, Antoine continued, crossing one leg and then the other. "We don't know how much time Marcus has, so we have to work quickly. We need to make sure that none of them have found their way to Seabrick and then leave immediately. We don't want to bring them to Piper's doorstep if we don't have to."

Wynn leaned forward on his knees, his usual nonchalance missing. "And what is the plan if dear Piper and Darren do not know anything? How will we go after Marcus?" He splayed his hands out in front of him.

Antoine ran a hand over his face and blew out a breath. It wasn't often we saw our leader so distraught and without a plan. "Then I suppose we have to look to our other contacts to find him." *Though, Morpheus might be the worst of the two.*

I gaped at him. "No way. You can't mean to go back to that bastard. He already tried to fuck me over once, and instead got Piper in the mix. We should figure it out on our own."

The others looked at me with my outburst, not quite catching up to who Antoine was thinking about. Then it clicked and they weren't any happier than I had been. Their shouts of protest overlapped each other until I couldn't tell who was saying what.

"After what he did to Piper? You can't be serious!"

"He'd more likely feed us to them than help us find them."

"Enough." The single word from Antoine quieted the whole limo. "This is not up for discussion. We do what we have to for our brother." His eyes locked on Wynn. "We agreed together when we fled Boris's that none of us would be left behind, ever."

A mumble of agreement ran through the limo.

"Fine. Then let's hope that Piper and Darren know something. Or there's at least a hunter around I can pound into." Drake smacked his fist against the palm of his other hand.

I knew how he felt. I could do with a good fight myself. Some way to blow off this growing ball of tension in my chest.

The limo pulled up to the house Darren and Piper had been living in. Or as Wynn told it, Piper owned. Something that didn't really surprise me. That woman had more drive in her than people gave her credit for. If she set her mind to it, then she could do anything.

Even in the moonlight, the house could only be described as cute. Definitely something Piper would pick out. Darren would have gone for something more modern and durable. Not something with red shingles and white shutters. All it needed was a white picket fence and it would be the typical cliché of human homes.

A single light shined in the window, the curtains hiding the darkened figured moving inside of the house.

"Maybe only one of us should go?" I glanced toward my brothers, all of them restless to get out of the limo. Their gazes turned to me. I lifted my shoulders. "I'm just saying. If all of us go in there now, she's going to think something is wrong and it might be easier to break the news if only one of us goes inside."

Before my brothers could protest, Antoine announced, "Rayne's right. I'll go. Wait here."

None of us had the chance to argue before Antoine was out of the car and halfway up the brick walkway. Little lanterns lit the path and cast shadows where Antoine moved. I tuned out my brothers and reached my mind toward the house. There was low murmuring and then...

Rayne. Get everyone the fuck in here.

If Antoine was cursing, then it had to be bad. I jolted up in my seat and reached for the door handle. "Come on, Antoine needs us now."

No one argued as we piled out of the limo and hurried up the front walkway. The door was unlocked, but Drake practically broke the door down trying to get inside first. However, he stopped in the entryway, making his brother run into the back of him. Wynn and I barely had time to stop ourselves from doing the same.

"Where's Piper?" Drake gaped at something in the living room. Allister pushed past him, giving us room to file in behind him. Sitting in an armchair with knitting needles in her hand was not Piper, but Gretchen, our cook.

"I'm confused." Allister stepped forward to Antoine, who stared down at the older woman. "I thought you were watching the house? Where are Piper and Darren?"

Antoine crossed his arms and glared down at Gretchen hard. "That is exactly what I'd like to know."

Had it been any other human, they would have been quaking in their seat from having a lethal vampire like Antoine scowling at them. Gretchen either was used to putting up with our shit or just was so old she didn't give a crap anymore.

Setting aside her knitting, Gretchen picked up the teacup and saucer on the end table. She took a long sip before sighing. "You weren't supposed to find out like this."

Dear Lord, did they really run off together after all?

The thought came from Wynn, and it made me wonder what exactly had gone on when he visited last.

"What?" Drake snapped. "What weren't we supposed to find out?"

"Darren and Piper ran off together, isn't it obvious?" Wynn sagged into the nearby couch, sadness coating his form. A mixture of thoughts swirled through his head—elation, disappointment, and regret.

Gretchen's brows rose. "Well, I don't know anything about that. They certainly went together, but if breaking into the vampire hunter's base counted as a lover's rendezvous, I've been doing it wrong." She chuckled to herself as the rest of us froze in terror.

"I'm sorry, Gretchen. I must have wax in my ear." Allister wiggled a finger in his ear and smiled. "But I thought you said that Piper and Darren went to infiltrate the hunter's base?"

Gretchen nodded matter-of-factly, sipping slowly from her cup. "Precisely."

Antoine didn't yell. He didn't scream or threaten to rip her head off. He simply closed his eyes and seemed to count to ten before opening them again and asking, "Gretchen, dear, how did they even find the hunter's base? We've been searching for months and have found nothing."

Her lips curled into a wicked grin. Disturbing to see on a woman of her age. "Why, I told them.”

Everyone but Antoine balked at her words. Was Gretchen a hunter?

No way that old broad is a hunter. She's like my grandma.

What. The. Fuck.

"I'm assuming you, Gretchen..." Antoine said her name slow and meaningful. "You somehow found out their location and passed the information on, and not because you're part of this heinous organization."

Gretchen's brows rose and then she burst out laughing. Setting down her teacup, she coughed through her laughter. "Oh, my, Master Antoine, you sure know how to make an old woman's day." She cleared her throat and shook her head. "No. I was a hellcat in my day, but I never did something so extreme as to hunt vampires."

"Then how did you find out their location?" Drake demanded, suspicion in his tone.

Amusement twinkled in Gretchen's eyes. "Some of those imbeciles were poking around the house, and when they questioned me, I stuck a tracker on them. Then I told Piper and Darren where they were."

Everyone in the room visibly relaxed. I understood. It was a relief to find out that someone we had cared for, trusted, and invited into our home hadn't betrayed us. There was already too much at stake right now to have to worry about trouble from within.

"What I don't understand, Gretchen," Antoine continued, keeping that low-level tone that was far scarier than if he'd yelled, "is why didn't you bring that information to me? Why bring it here to Piper and Darren?"

Gretchen shrugged a shoulder. "You have enough on your hands. Besides, it was safer to come to them than it was to find you. What they did with the information...well, I can't be held responsible for that."

Drake growled and punched a nearby wall. The plaster broke and crumbled to the ground. "Well, I don't like it. Why the fuck would she think it was a good idea?"

"Hey, watch it. This is Piper's house. She's going to be pissed." I pointed at Drake and scowled.

Allister turned to his brother. "What makes you think it was Piper's idea?"

Drake snorted. "Only she would be stupid enough to do something so rash. She's always putting herself in harm's way for us. We don't die that easily. She's human."

"A superhuman now, to be technical," I added with an incline of my head. "She's got a bigger chance of blending in than us."

"But those guys are hardcore killers, trained in weapons, martial arts, and who knows what else!" Drake threw his hands up in the air and stalked around the room. "I just don't understand how she thought she wouldn't be found out."

Perhaps, she didn't. Wynn thought.

I turned to Wynn. "What do you mean?"

Wynn lounged back on the couch and cocked his head to the side. "When I was here last, Piper was...different."

Antoine's brows furrowed. "Different how?"

Wynn's lips ticked up at the edges, and his hands came out in front of him like he was cupping something in his hands. "Her body no longer had that supple feel to it. It was lean, hard, that of someone who had been using their muscles far more than an average maid."

Drake's face hardened and his lips pressed into a thoughtful frown. "You're saying that you think Piper's been preparing for this all year? How could we have missed this?"

"We've kind of been busy." Allister gave a helpless shrug. "It's likely we've missed a lot."

Before we could get any further into it, the doorbell rang. Five heads turned toward the door.

"That better be Piper coming to grovel for our forgiveness," Drake snarled, stomping toward the door.

I snickered. "In your dreams. Besides, why would she be ringing her own doorbell?"

Allister, Drake, and I crowded around the front door as Drake opened it. A tall human man stood on the other side, holding a bouquet of roses and what smelled like soup inside of the paper bag he carried. When the man saw the three of us, his face went white and he shifted on the front porch.

"Uh, this is Piper Billings' home, isn't it?" If he'd been wearing a necktie, he would have been pulling at it right now. *Fuck, what are they doing here? Doesn't she know any ugly guys?*

Drake's lips curled into a cruel smirk. "Yes, it is. Who may I say is asking?"

The man licked his lips and stumbled over his words. He stopped and breathed. *Get a hold of yourself, Jack. You're the Big Man, remember? Hotshot lawyer. These guys have nothing on you.* I stifled a chuckle. "I'm Jack Biggs, Piper's boss."

Drake leaned against one side of the doorframe and cocked a brow. "And do you usually come by your employee's home at," he glanced at the watch on his wrist, "nine o'clock at night? With flowers and food?"

Allister crowded in next to him, but I was comfortable standing back to watch the scene unfold before me. Though Wynn and Antoine weren't at the door, I could feel them shift in this direction, no doubt listening in.

Jack 'the Big Man' frowned at them. "No, but I do bring flowers when I was an ass and need to apologize. The soup is for the flu. Isn't she sick?"

Drake froze and then he dropped his arms to his side. *Fuck. What do I say?*

I sighed and pushed between the twins. "Piper's too sick for visitors, but we'll tell her you stopped by. Thanks." I grabbed the flowers and bag from his hands and backed into the house.

"But I wanted to—"

Drake shut the door in the lawyer's face.

"So, that's Piper's boss?" Allister mused, scratching his chin.

I snorted. "That guy's not her boss. He's the 'Big Man.'" I cackled all the way back into the living room where our real problems were.

Chapter 8

Piper

TRISTAN WAS AS CHATTY as they came. At least, for a vampire hunter. He'd done nothing but talk my ear off the whole tour of the headquarters. I'd seen the rec room, the weapon galley—which, coincidentally, was not the wall of torture devices in the common area—and the kitchen. All that was left were some offices and the sleeping accommodations. That, to my disappointment, were little more than soldiers' barracks. Everyone slept in a tiny bunk bed that didn't even constitute as a twin.

Looked like finding some privacy to report in was close to nil. I'd have to figure out something else.

"I'm bunking here." Tristan pointed to his spot on the bottom bunk three rows into the first room. Yep, there were rows. Each bunk had its own footlocker and that was it. Nothing else. Apparently, the hunters were akin to monks, minus the celibacy based on the way Tristan kept eyeballing me like a cupcake whenever he thought I wasn't looking.

I grunted in response. It was my go-to answer. I didn't want to talk too much. I knew myself, and if pressured, I'd spill my guts like a newbie on their first sea voyage. Tristan didn't seem to take offense to my lack of answers, so I decided to stick with it.

"You could take the one next to me..." Tristan rubbed the back of his head, pointing toward a bed one bunk over.

I took the crossbow off my back and sat it on the bed before sitting next to it. I bounced a little bit to see if it was softer than it looked. No such luck. Might as well be sleeping on a rock.

"The last person died during the raid in Paris. If it hasn't been picked over— "

"Paris?" I perked up, my brows rising. "Like France?"

Tristan smiled, dimples appearing in his cheeks. "No, sorry. Texas. We don't get many destination places. Vampires tend to gravitate toward smaller towns. Easier to hide out. Frankfurt was one of the biggest raids we've had in a while."

I grunted again.

"Anyway…" Tristan moved over to the footlocker. "You can put your stuff in here." He lifted the lock on the locker with a frown before dropping it. Then he kicked the lock with his heavy boots and the lock clattered to the floor. I made a startled sound in my throat but then covered it with a cough. Flipping the lid, he shuffled something around inside. "You can have whatever they left behind or trash it." He lifted a pair of fuzzy handcuffs with a grin before twirling them around one finger.

My lips ticked up.

He pointed the cuffs toward a box on the wall at the beginning of the room. "That's the donation box. You can put whatever you don't want in there." He winked and folded the handcuffs up before tucking them into his back pocket.

"So..." Tristan trailed off as if unable to think of something else to keep himself there longer. "Chow time is at eighteen hundred hours. Breakfast is at oh seven hundred. Feel free to find me if you need anything." He pointed toward his bunk. "You know where to find me."

I inclined my head.

Seeing that I wasn't going to continue the conversation, Tristan nodded back and headed toward the barracks' door. At the last moment, I realized something. Something that had been bugging me.

"Uh, hey, Tristan." I stood and jogged the few feet to catch up to him. Tristan stopped and turned back to me, hope springing into his eyes. "Uh, do you know if they brought back anyone from Frankfurt? Another vampire?"

Tristan's brow furrowed. "No, they killed them all. Except for the nest they're still hunting. Even that creepy ancient vamp." His lips curled up at the edges. "You know, I heard he looked more monster than human. With clubbed hands and fangs down to his chin." He put his fingers up to his face like fangs.

I chuckled. "Not clubbed, but good. Good. That's good."

"You saw him?" Tristan's brows raised.

Crap. This was why I grunted.

"Uh, yeah, briefly. But I was chasing down one of the other bloodsuckers." I hated to talk about the guys like that, but if I was going to do this, I had to go all the way. "But it's good to know that demon is really dead." I shuddered and it wasn't fake.

A heavy hand sat on my shoulder and my head whipped up. "I get it. This job is hard sometimes. It's best when the demon looks like what they are." His eyes grew dark, his mind going somewhere else. "It's harder when they look like fallen angels with hair the color of spun gold and eyes so green, emeralds were jealous. They make you feel so lucky to just be in their presence." He sighed and shook his head, and whatever memory that had held him cleared from his eyes.

"Yeah." I patted him on the arm as well, my heart full of emotion. "I've been there."

"But," Tristan's face hardened, "in the end, they're all demons. Some just wear a pretty mask. They all deserve one thing."

"What's that?"

"A stake through the heart." Tristan ended with a finality that chilled my blood. "Anyway," his expression brightened and he squeezed my shoulder, "I'll let you know when the vamp gets here and then the real fun begins."

I forced a smile. "Thanks."

When Tristan left, I raced toward the bathroom. Shoving a toilet stall open, my stomach revolted against me. When I'd thrown up everything I had in it, I swiped my hand over my forehead and sank down onto the floor by the toilet.

This was a lot harder than I thought. Not only did I have to find a way to get my guys off their radar, but I had to rescue one of my own. It hurt my heart to think that they were hurting one of the guys right now and that I would have to witness it soon.

I didn't know if I could do this.

Sighing, I shakily got to my feet and pushed open the stall door. Slowly moving to the sink, I flicked on the tap. I wet my hands and rubbed them over my face and the back of my neck before shuffling back to my bunk. My hard as a rock bed was looking mighty fine, but the still open footlocker at the end drew my attention.

Sitting on the floor, I bent over the box. Besides the handcuffs Tristan had taken—cringe—there were a few other illicit items. I smirked, pulling out a leather riding crop. I could think of quite a few things I could use this for. Putting it to the side, I grabbed the next item. Assless chaps, no thank you. Though…Drake and Allister would look great in these. I added them to the keep pile.

A huge bottle of lube. My eyes widened before putting it with the other stuff. Hey, I was dating multiple guys, couldn't hurt to have extra.

Once I got through all the dirty things, I found actual useful items. A blade with a serrated edge. It wasn't as nice as the ones Billy had given me, but you could never have to many weapons.

The rest of the stuff was pretty much the usual personal items. Toiletries. A hairbrush. A box of lemon-flavored condoms. The vampire hunter handbook.

I did a double-take. "Seriously?" I muttered to myself, as I flipped the book over in my hand. "They actually have a handbook?" I looked around the empty barracks and then to the clock on the wall. Most of them would be at chow now, so I figured I still had a bit before they came back and I'd have to fake more, but I didn't want to risk it. I put the book in my keep pile and went through the rest of the items. I threw most of them in the giveaway pile, but a few things I kept. Like the oversized t-shirt that I planned on sleeping in. While the leather pants made me look hot, there was no fucking way I was going to try and sleep in them.

Shoving all the things I wanted to keep back into the box, sans the vampire hunter handbook, I carried the get-rid-ofs over to the donation box. Dropping them in, I thought about going down to dinner. My stomach rolled in protest. Nope. I was far to stressed out to eat right now. I'd just grab something for breakfast.

Quickly changing into my new shirt, I folded up my clothes and put them in my locker. I didn't have a lock for it, so I'd have to hope no one would go digging in it with me a few feet away.

I put my gun under my pillow for safe keeping and then slid under the itchy covers of my cot. I rolled over and curled up into a ball on my side. I punched the pillow a few times, pushing it up into a semi-comfortable shape, then rolled onto my back. Then my side again.

Damn. I missed my bed back home.

But what was home? The Durand house? Or the one in Seabrick?

While living with Darren had been great, I still missed the others. Every day felt like a battle to keep going. I wanted nothing more than to have my guys around me once more. So, I guess even if that was in the cottage in

Seabrick or the mansion, I couldn't truly feel like I was home without them there.

I sighed and closed my eyes, trying to force myself to drift off. If I was going to have to face one of my guys being tortured tomorrow, I was going to need my rest.

Thankfully, it didn't take as long as I expected to fall asleep. My mind and body were worn out from all the lying and risking my life. Unfortunately, though, my dreams decided I didn't need to have a peaceful escape from my danger-filled existence.

In my mind, I chased after Tristan, demanding he take me to the captured vampire. When he finally brought me to him, I find all six of the vampires and Darren chained on a wall. Why Darren was even in there, I had no clue, but apparently my subconscious knew something I didn't. Whatever that maybe, I found myself being told to pick which one should live. Because I could only have one. Such utter bullshit. Nowhere did it say I had to pick one and I refused to pick, even if a dream told me I had to.

"Piper."

I jerked awake, my gun somehow already in my hand.

"Woah, it's just me, Tristan." The smiling face of the big vampire hunter stared down at me. "A bit jumpy, aren't you?"

I lowered my gun. "Sorry."

"No worries. It's not like we don't live with vampire hunters." He winked. "I just thought you'd like to know they brought the vamp in."

That had me sitting up. "Yes, I do. Thanks."

Tristan backed away from my bunk, giving me room to climb out of bed. He made a choking sound that made me realize I was only wearing the large shirt and no pants.

Determined to be the badass that I was pretending to be, I stood from the bed and pushed past him to get my clothes from my footlocker, acutely aware of his eyes on me the whole time. If it had been one of the guys, I'd be beet red right now or flaunting it a lot more, depending on who was looking. However, since Tristan wasn't one of them, I grabbed my clothes and made for the bathroom without sparing him a glance.

The bathroom, to my displeasure, was filled to the brim with other hunters. Since the bathroom was coed, there were men at the urinals and women primping at the mirrors. I got a few curious looks as I hurried into the first empty stall, but no one stopped me.

I changed out of my sleeping shirt and into my leather pants faster than I'd ever been able to before. Last time it'd taken Darren's help to get them on, which while that had been hilarious, it would be humiliating if I had to ask a hunter for a hand. The prospect of that had me into my pants in record time. With my shirt and daggers backed on, I pushed out of the stall and stalked out of the bathroom.

Not saying anything, I stopped by Tristan. I contemplated taking the crossbow as well with my daggers and gun but seeing as no one else was that loaded down with weapons decided against it.

Tristan looked up from the book in his hand, a worn copy of the same book in my footlocker, and asked, "Ready?"

I grunted, crossing my arms over my chest.

"You know, I like a woman of few words," Tristan mentioned conversationally, as we made our way down one of the long hallways of the manor. "You know, most women would be going on and on about where they'd come from or bragging about their latest kill. You, though, you have a bit of mystery to you." He winked in my direction.

True to my character, I grunted and suppressed the urge to roll my eyes. Mystery, right.

"You have no idea how many of the guys are gossiping about you. Trying to figure out where you came from." Tristan glanced over at me from the corner of his eye, but I avoided meeting his gaze.

"How much farther?" The anticipation was killing me. I didn't know who they had, but I knew whoever it ended up being, I wouldn't be relieved until they were back home safely. Who knew that my going undercover as a vampire hunter would end up like this? I didn't know how much I could do to help whoever got captured, but I would do my damnedest to get them free.

"We have to go down in the basement," Tristan explained, as we descended the stairs. "That's where we keep all the vampires." His brows furrowed. "It's in the handbook."

I didn't meet his stare, keeping my eyes forward. "I don't stay in one place long. Prefer to keep moving."

"Ah, one of those kinds. We have a few like that." Tristan puffed up his chest with a macho grunt. "I consider myself a lone hunter as well. Nothing beats hunting down bloodsuckers with only yourself for backup.

Know what I'm saying?" He nudged me with an elbow and I gave a weak smile.

We rounded the common area and went through the kitchens. My stomach rumbled in protest, so I snatched an apple off a nearby counter. No one called foul, so I bit into it with abandon. When we stopped before a metal door, I swallowed hard. This was it.

"It's exciting, isn't it?" Tristan grinned broadly, rubbing his hands together. "The anticipation of seeing a vampire up close and personal. Where we are the predator rather than the prey." His whole muscled body shuddered. "It's enough to get a guy hyped up."

Suddenly, the apple in my stomach fought against me. Hearing Tristan talk about vampires that way, especially my guys, made me question humanity as a whole. He spoke of them like they were just animals without intelligence or feelings. Even though there were some vampires—Boris and Valentine—who deserved what came to them, there were others who hadn't done anything to cause the hunters to track them down like helpless prey. My vampire knowledge was limited to the guys and the other nasties I'd encountered, so it wasn't like I knew all vampires were good or bad.

But there had to be others like the Durands. I couldn't believe that they were the only vampires who cared for more than themselves.

Tristan turned the doorknob with a wicked gleam in his eyes. While he was excited about whatever lay down below, I was freaking the fuck out. I didn't sign up for this. I didn't want to see one of my guys, one of the people I loved, tortured and maimed. I wasn't confident I could hold back my reaction when I saw them. That I wouldn't attack whoever was closest, likely Tristan, to get my guy and get out of there.

The stairway was dark and dank, the only light shining was from the kitchen and what little light was on down below. Each step down the stairs made my heart rate ratchet up a bit. It got to the point where I was holding my breath by time we got to the bottom of the stairs. I blinked into the dimly lit room, my eyes adjusting as I forced myself to breathe so I didn't pass out.

"Ah, there it is." Tristan chuckled, his body blocking my view of the vampire who grunted and moaned. The clank of metal told me they'd chained him up, and I feared what else they might have done. I almost didn't want to see. I was tempted to run back upstairs and keep the image of my loved one hurt and tortured out of my head, but I couldn't.

Forcing one foot in front of the other, I pushed past Tristan and focused my gaze on the huddled, bloodied figure on the floor. I knew immediately who it was. The buzzed, dark hair on his head, the strong jawline, and muscles bigger than Tristan's all gave away his identity. The one vampire who, while I hadn't gotten to know him as well as the others, still squeezed my heart to see him like this.

Marcus.

Chapter 9

Marcus

EVERYTHING ACHED. THE HUNTERS hadn't just knocked me out, but they had taken great pleasure in beating me within an inch of my immortal life.

Footsteps fell on the stairs leading to God knew where, pulling my attention away from the pain. Two sets of them. One of them male, the other...female? They were lighter, almost hesitant.

It wasn't that I was surprised to see a female hunter. I'd been knocked out by one. I just didn't expect one to come to taunt me. Since I'd arrived at this new base, only men had come down to check on me, spit on me, and sometimes wave their bloody wrists in front of me as they laughed. No women though.

Except now.

"We keep it chained up, but not sedated," a gruff voice explained to the female. It. I had been downgraded from a fearsome monster to an it. Oh, if the other knights could see me now.

"Is that safe?" the woman asked, my head too fuzzy with hunger to pick her voice apart.

"It's too weak to break the chains. We haven't fed it since it was captured, and apparently they haven't been eating regularly either. Which was a bonus on our part. Made our job easier." The man chuckled and the woman grunted. "This one doesn't have any special powers, so you don't have to worry about it putting you in its thrall."

I almost laughed. So that's why they hadn't sent females. They thought I was like Wynn or Drake who could ensnare others with a single look. Sadly for them, they had their intel wrong. It didn't matter if they were male or female. Their powers didn't discriminate. Unfortunately, none of that helped me right now.

"Don't get too close, it's still dangerous. But then you'd know that, huh?" The male laughed as the woman stepped forward. She crouched down before me and beneath the oily scent of the male there was another smell, a sweeter fragrance. Why was it so familiar? It was almost like...like...strawberries and coffee grounds. The revelation made my eyes snap open.

Big, light brown eyes stared down at me with a mixture of horror and sadness. I jolted up, ignoring the pain in my limbs and head. Piper. What the hell was she doing here? My eyes skimmed over her outfit, the daggers at her hips. She had gone undercover.

Had this been Antoine's idea? Had he sent her to save me? No. He'd never put her in danger that way and Piper had the audacity to think up such a plan on her own. I almost laughed. If Antoine didn't know yet, he would be beyond pissed when he found out. I didn't want to be Piper when Antoine got his hands on her.

"What are you smiling at, bloodsucker?" The man scowled, stepping closer to Piper. "She smells good, doesn't she? But you can't have her." The male's hand clamped down on her shoulder, but she didn't lift her gaze from me.

My hackles raised over his hand on her. She didn't belong to him either. A low growl rumbled from the back of my throat and I didn't know how I had the energy, but I yanked on my chains, jerking forward and glaring at the male hunter.

"Watch it." The male hunter tried to pull her away, but Piper shook her head, not budging an inch.

"I'm fine. He won't hurt me." The sound of her voice was like heavenly bells in my ears.

"I know you're used to being in the middle of the vamps, but it doesn't mean you can be reckless." He urged her once more to back away.

Piper stared at me with pain in her eyes. Was that for me? Then, with a watery smile, she pushed up off her thighs and stood. Her face changed instantly. The empathy and sadness there shifted into a hardened mask. I'd never seen Piper put on a face so fast. She'd always been open and honest. It caused an ache in my chest for this gorgeous woman to have been damaged in such a way because of us.

It was because of us. From the moment Piper had walked into our house, she had damned herself. She'd been attacked, kidnapped, and now forced to be someone she wasn't all for the sake of being involved with us. I wished she would have never come to work for us, then maybe she wouldn't be putting herself in such danger. Especially not for me. I wasn't worth it. I'd already been damned from the moment Boris changed me. He should have killed me that first night. Saved us all the trouble.

My eyes followed her as she walked up the stairs behind the male hunter, not allowing him to shield her from me. Five steps up, she paused and turned to look behind her. The agony in her gaze pulled at me, but I couldn't let her risk her safety. I flicked my head toward the stairs, insisting that she go. With a tight jaw, she did as she was told—a first. The others wouldn't believe me when I told them. If I got to tell them. At this rate, I wasn't sure I'd make it to the next night, let alone to see my brothers again. As I sagged against the wall, I let Piper's face hover in my mind as my eyes grew heavy with exhaustion. At least I got to see Piper's face one more time.

I woke from the slam of a door above. Multiple booted feet pounded down the stairs. I cracked my eyes open, counting the hunters as they lined up around me. At least six of them. Each of them wore a menacing look on their face. It was a far cry from Piper's empathetic gaze.

In some ways, I was thankful for it. Hating them and the fight for survival was almost better than the ache in my chest from watching her see me this way. It wasn't anything I would wish upon anyone else. However, for whatever reason she was here, and I couldn't stop her from seeing it. I could, however, keep the sadistic bastards before me from getting my brothers.

"Oh, you're back," I rasped, my mouth and throat dry, the lack of blood making it hard to speak. "I was beginning to worry."

"Shut up, vampire." The head of this group of hunters kicked a booted foot out and hit me in the chest. Pain splintered from the impact. Had I been human, that one kick would have broken a rib or something. Unfortunately for me, I was made of sturdier stuff. I'd have to push them further to get them to do what I wanted.

I gathered my strength and forced a smile to my lips. "P-Pussy."

A few of the hunters chuckled, causing their leader to turn red with rage. Fists swung as he pounded into me. Hitting my face over and over again. My fangs ached to feed, my mouth watering at the taste of my own blood. The hunter continued to wail on me, breaking my nose at one point, and my eyes began to swell. I thought I might actually have gotten what I wanted, but before the hunter could really lay into me, one of the others pulled him back.

"Hold up, Huss. The boss wants him alive to question him. If you kill him now, we lose any chance of finding the others."

"Don't you think I know that?" Huss, I assumed, snarled. The room dimmed, my eyes too swollen to see clearly. "It's immortal. It won't die from a little beating." Huss paused and then asked in a low voice, "Or would you rather take its place?"

The man swallowed thickly, and stuttered out, "N-No. No, sir."

"Then why don't you go fuck off, I have work to do." Several of the men laughed at Huss's words before he turned back to me.

The man who'd stopped him didn't speak again as Huss and the others kicked and punched me. Spouting insults and literally spitting on me. Some part of me, the part that still thought he was a knight of God's army believed I deserved this. I was a monster. A creature of darkness and death. This was God's punishment for letting myself go astray. I deserved everything they gave me and more.

Please. Kill me. End this eternity and keep Piper safe.

I had no doubt that she wouldn't leave me here to die. She would do everything in her power to save me, and I couldn't let her. I wouldn't snuff her light out to save my cursed one. She deserved more than that.

They'd unchained me to get better access to my softer body parts. By the time they were done with me, I was a quivering, aching mass of flesh. I couldn't even lift my head to antagonize them to finish the job.

Huss dropped down to my level, his fingers digging into my skin as he grabbed me by the back of the neck. "Not so tough now, huh? Stick around," he breathed in my face, "we're just getting started." He released me without warning and my face smacked against the concrete beneath me. The sound of their booted feet leaving lulled me into the darkness where I hoped to stay.

I didn't dream. I was too beaten and starved to have the energy to conjure up any kind of subconscious thought. Though, I thought I was dreaming when I heard the door at the top of the stairs open and a soft set of steps came down to stop before me.

"Oh, Marcus." Piper's soft voice filled my ears and I tried to force myself awake.

No. No. She couldn't be here. She needed to go. To leave before they caught her.

Soft hands touched my face, making me wince. "Oh, I'm sorry, but I need to clean you up," Piper explained, as she pushed me over onto my back. "I don't have a lot of time. The others went to some big speaking event with the president. Can you believe they treat this guy like he's the actual leader of the country rather than their little world?" she scoffed and shook her head.

"G-Go." I coughed out the word, trying to get her to leave. If they caught her here, they'd do worse to her than to me.

Piper, the stubborn woman, huffed and pulled a plastic container out. A wrapper crinkled as she messed with it before something cold and stinging touched the bloody split in my lip. She wiped gently over my face. Every place she touched burned, but just her presence was a balm on my soul which was far more damaged than my body.

"They really beat the crap out of you, huh?" Piper murmured, more to herself than to me. I sagged on the ground, letting her do what she willed, regardless of it being pointless. I'd die at the end of all this, and I just wanted to do so without killing her or my brothers in the process.

She leaned back on her heels and sighed. "This isn't working. You've lost too much blood and I can't imagine they're feeding you." Piper shifted around, muttering to herself. When her weight settled on my hips, my eyes widened. "Oh, don't look at me like that. I'm not going to ravish you in this state." My lips twitched, but it hurt too much to smile. "You need blood. I'm going to give it to you."

I shook my head, or tried to. While my body wanted to push her away, my fangs pulsated at the thought of sinking into Piper's tender flesh. She was right. I needed blood, but the problem was I wasn't sure once I started, I'd be able to stop.

Piper, sensing my distress, stared down at me with a soft smile as she pulled her blonde hair to the side. "Don't worry. I trust you. I'll make you stop."

With strength I didn't think she had, Piper dipped her arm under me and lifted my torso up to meet her. She pressed my face to her neck. I wished I could say I had the strength to pull away, to tell her no and die in peace, but if I had proven anything in my long, immortal life, it was that I didn't have the strength to deny anyone anything. Least of all her.

The pulse in her neck teased and taunted me, making my fangs push at the back of my lips. My mouth opened on its own accord, and before I could give her any warning of the pain that would come with the action, my fangs sank into her. Sweet, sweet nectar of life spilled into my mouth. Piper cried out slightly but didn't pull back from me. Not that I would have let her anyway. Just that single drop of blood was enough for my body to go into survival mode. One arm wrapped around her waist, pulling her closer to me as the other held onto her head. Piper no longer needed to hold me up, my strength returning and my wounds healing with each sip of her glorious life force.

Her body pressed to mine, the soft curves of her form pushing up against my chest and hips. It was no wonder my body woke up enough to harden my cock beneath her. A small moan came from her throat and her thighs squeezed my hips, startling me enough to pull back from her neck, staring down at her enraptured expression.

Piper's eyes were closed, her head thrown back, and her mouth gaping in an O shape. It almost seemed like she enjoyed my bite. Which was ridiculous. I was near starved to death and I couldn't have been gentle with her, but when I scented the air it was there, the telltale hint of arousal mixed in with her normal scent.

"Why'd you stop?" Piper's almond-colored eyes blinked up at me. "Did you get enough?"

I swallowed and grunted, nodding stiffly. "Yes. Thank you." After a long awkward moment, I added, "You should get out of here."

"Yeah, give me a second." Piper licked her lips and shifted in my lap. I forced myself not to react to the brush of her heat against my length. It had been so long since I'd found myself aroused by anyone. Least of all in a situation like this one. Piper had surprised me in more than one way in the time I'd known her. That my body wanted her even now shouldn't really shock me.

Her hands went to her neck and it came away red, blood still trickling from the bite wound. "Do you think you could...you know?" She angled her head to the side, giving me a clear view of where I'd bitten her. I'd really gone to town on her neck and my asshole of a self didn't even heal her properly.

"Of course." I ducked my head and my tongue dipped out, sliding over her skin as I lapped up the escaping blood. Piper's fingers curled into my shirt at the sides, and her hips jerked against mine. I licked and lapped at her neck until it was completely healed, but didn't move away just yet. Having sated the hunger in my stomach, another hunger came alive. My hands sank to her hips, pulling her against me with a grunt as I continued to press my tongue to her skin.

Piper's hips swirled on top of me, but then she seemed to catch herself, pulling away from me. "I think it's healed now. Thank you."

Reluctantly, I lifted my head from her neck. Our faces hovered close to one another, the minty scent of her breath meeting my nose, making me self-conscious of the blood that no doubt covered my face and saturated my breath. I shifted to pull away, but a hand touched the back of my head and my brows rose in question.

Piper stared at my lips, a curious expression on her face. "Can I just...try something?"

My head jerked in agreement, but I didn't move as she leaned forward. Her mouth captured my bottom lip, suckling the taste of herself from my skin. My cock jumped in my pants as I fought for control. Piper's tongue, wet and warm, slid over my lips and then burrowed into my mouth.

This wasn't the time or place for this. The hunters could be coming down here at any moment to question me, and they'd see Piper had healed me and it would put her in further danger. However, the feel of her mouth on mine was too much to ignore.

I flipped us so she was beneath me on the ground and took control of the kiss. My hips thrust against her core and a startled moan slid from her throat. I swallowed it down as my tongue searched every crevice of her mouth, tasting her, memorizing every inch of her. If I was going to die soon, I wanted to die with the taste of her in my mouth and a smile on my face.

Piper pulled back to breathe, but it only caused me to drop my mouth to the exposed skin of the low neckline she wore. I grazed my fangs against one mound, making Piper hiss as I broke then skin and then lapped it up.

"Marcus," she groaned, her hands tangled in my hair. "We can't. We're gonna get caught."

I paused long enough to cock my head to the side, listening to the sounds from above. "There's no one in the house. At least not inside." I turned a wicked grin back on her, pushing my hips against her core. "We can." I hesitated for a moment, a thought coming to me. "I mean, if you want to."

Piper blinked up at me. "I do...I do...it's just you're still healing, and these leather pants weren't the easiest to get on."

I stared down at her for a long moment and then threw my head back and laughed. Leaning down, I murmured, "Then why don't we move this somewhere more...not here." Backing away from her, I stood up and offered her a hand. "How about it? Ready for a jailbreak?"

Chapter 10

Piper

I WORRIED THE WHOLE day about him and almost gave myself away several times with Tristan and numerous other hunters who thought it would be a good idea to get to know the new girl.

When I heard they were going to interrogate the prisoner, I practically died in my seat. I didn't have to be there to know they were going to hurt him. However, if I was down there, I didn't trust myself not to throw myself between him and them. So, I sat upstairs while Tristan and his friend regaled me with their latest hunt, all while my stomach rolled and my mind whirled at what they could be doing to him.

The group of hunters came back up shortly after. It had taken everything in me not to rush down to the basement and check on him. He must have been hurting, not to mention starving. I forced myself to sit there until Tristan and the others announced it was time to go see the president.

When they headed for the front door and not to some other part of the manor, I frowned. "Where are we going?"

"The president loves to have a crowd for his talks. He can't do that here in the manor since we have most of it full of weapons and other equipment." Tristan bent low, his hand touching my back. He'd gotten a little more handsy since we first went to see Marcus. I wasn't sure if he thought I was softer than I looked and now it was okay to come on to me, but I didn't like it.

"So we're going outside?" My eyes narrowed on the dim light coming through the windows. It was almost dusk now, and I wanted to check on Marcus when it was fully dark. If I was going to get him out of here, I had to do it soon. I didn't have much of a plan after that, but I'd have to figure it out along the way.

"We have an auditorium built in the back of the manor for this very reason." Tristan chuckled at my appalled expression. "I know, it seems like a lot for one guy, but what can you do? He's the boss."

I hummed, keeping my opinion to myself.

If they put this much effort into keeping their leader happy, I didn't know how they ever thought for themselves. The longer I stayed in the vampire hunters' base, the more I felt like they were just one big hive with a single common goal—kill all vampires and anyone associated with vampires.

It made me really happy they hadn't killed Gretchen. Though, now I was more worried about why they had spared her over if it was actually part of their rules. I needed to find time to read over that handbook before I got much further into this.

Following the horde of hunters out of the manor, I began to concoct a plan. While they were busying bowing down or taking shots of his greatness, whatever the hunters did to get riled up, I'd go save Marcus. It'd be tricky, because if they caught me leaving with him, then not only would he be taken once more but my cover would be blown.

There were far more hunters here than I thought before. Most of the hunters must have been out in the field because the auditorium area, which had to seat at least a hundred, was filled to the brim. I took a chair in the back with Tristan, content to watch the others than to be up close and personal with their president. Who knew if this guy could tell I wasn't the real deal or not?

"Isn't this exciting? We're going to get to see him," a female hunter in the row in front of us squealed, her hands clasped together in front of her. It was really peculiar to hear a bloodthirsty vampire hunter fangirling so hard over their president. It wasn't like he was the real president or even anyone famous.

Tristan snorted next to me. "They act like the man has a thrall of his own with the way the women carry on about President Vincent." He shook his head, but there was a sense of excitement coming off him that he couldn't hide from me.

I grunted in agreement, sort of curious now to see what this President Vincent looked like. If they were this hyped up for him, then there had to be something extraordinary about him. However, while I wanted to see the man in question, I had to take this chance to get Marcus out. Since all the hunters were going to be enthralled, as Tristan said, with this Vincent person, this might be my one and only chance to get him out.

"I'll be back," I murmured to Tristan. "I want to get a better look."

Tristan sighed but didn't stop me as the crowd of hunters roared and someone stepped out of the side of the stage. While everyone's eyes were forward, I darted the opposite way of the platform and backtracked up the stairs and toward the manor.

The clapping and screaming for President Vincent almost drowned out the pounding of my pulse in my ears. I couldn't waste this chance. I had to get Marcus out of here.

I hadn't expected to take things as far as we did. I knew he was going to need blood and was fully prepared to donate to the cause. I didn't know if it was because I was a human servant now or maybe my hormones were all out of whack still, something I'd have to ask Darren about later, but Marcus's fangs in my neck hadn't hurt as much as I'd expected. It actually felt sort of good. Then, there was the grinding and I didn't know what exactly came over me, but for some reason kissing Marcus seemed like the logical thing to do.

"How about it? Ready for a jailbreak?" The way Marcus looked at me made my toes curl and my panties liquefy. I never thought this stoic man could turn me on so much, but now that he had, it's like something inside him had changed. Or maybe he was blood drunk and that made him less reserved with his words.

"Hold up, back up now." I held my hands up and shook my head. "I'm all for getting out of here, but I still have a job to do."

Marcus's brows furrowed. "You didn't come here to save me?"

The disappointment on his face was so adorable, I really hated to burst his bubble.

When I saw Marcus down here, I thought part of me would be relieved that it wasn't one of the other guys, but it tore me up inside so much that I almost said fuck it and tried to save him right then and there with Tristan beside me. However, I knew there were tons of hunters above at the moment, and I wouldn't make it out of the basement, let alone the whole manor.

"Sorry, but no." I glanced toward the door and then back to Marcus. "I'm here on my own. I just found out they had caught one of you guys yesterday. You're lucky I was already in here to help you out or you'd be dust on the floor by now."

Marcus frowned. "Does Antoine know you're here?"

I arched a brow. "What do you think?"

Shaking his head, he gave me one of his rare smiles. "He's going to kill you, and me for that matter. Come on, we got to get out of here." He grabbed my elbow, but I pulled away from him.

"No. I can't leave." I pushed at Marcus. "You have to leave. If I leave, they'll think I had a hand in it and ruin the whole point of this."

"If you come with us, then it won't matter if they know," he argued with a growl. His head tipped up toward the ceiling. "There's movement up above. We have to go. Now."

I pulled my daggers free, leaning back into a fighting stance. "I said, no. I'm going to do what I came here to do. You go. I'll think of something." I chewed on my lower lip for a second, and then without warning, I slashed out with my blade, slicing Marcus on the arm. "Bite me," I urged him when I, too, heard voices.

"What? I don't think this is the time."

"Ugh, I don't mean like that. Just bite and run. That way they think you attacked me. If they find me here unharmed and you gone, they'll know I did it." I leaned my head to the side and stepped up to him. "Hurry, now."

Marcus gave me an unsure look. I was pretty sure he was regretting that kiss now, but he did as I asked. As quick as lightning, he struck my neck, biting me but not taking any more blood. With a brief caress of my cheek, he murmured, "Antoine really is going to kill me now," before he disappeared up the stairs.

There was a startled sound above, but there must not have been many hunters up there because there wasn't much of a struggle. Ignoring what was going on upstairs, since Marcus could handle it from here, I used my daggers to tear the sleeve of my shirt and dug into the bite to make some of the blood trickle out. Throwing one dagger across the room, I dropped to my knees and eased down onto my front, chucking my other dagger a few feet away so it looked like I'd been trying for it.

The door to the basement burst open and the pounding of feet made me close my eyes and relax onto the ground. I played dead like my life depended on it, which it did.

"Fuck!" a growling voice yelled as they came down the last few steps to where I lay. "Vincent's going to kick our asses."

A hand touched my back and I groaned. "Hey, she's alive!" the person above me called to their companion. They rolled me over and looked me over. "Looks like he didn't take that much blood from her."

"What was she doing down here?" the other voice asked with a hint of disbelief and annoyance.

"Doesn't matter, we better get her to the infirmary before she bleeds out," the first guy said before arms slipped beneath me, picking me up. The person holding me smelled like salami and goat cheese, a toxic combination that made me hold my breath.

They carried me up the stairs and into the kitchen. A sharp inhale told me Tristan had come into the room. "Piper! Fuck, Bishop, what happened to her?"

"You know this woman?" Bishop, the guy carrying me, questioned. "We found her down in the basement. The creature has escaped." The suspicion in his voice was clear, but to my relief and surprise Tristan stuck up for me.

"You don't think she let him go, do you?" Tristan snarled, no longer the big teddy bear guy he'd shown me earlier. "She's bleeding and unconscious, for God's sake!"

"It could be a trick." Bishop tightened his grip on me. "She shows up a few days before the vampire, and now he's missing? I don't think so."

"Why don't you make sure she doesn't die first before judging her," Tristan argued, his arm going under me as well. "Here, let someone who actually cares if she dies, take her to the infirmary."

"Here's her daggers." The other voice from down below said.

"Thanks," Tristan grunted.

"I have to make a report to Vincent," Bishop declared, far happier about that task than keeping me alive.

Tristan held me tight, and a jerk in his shoulders signaled his nod. "Do what you have to do, and I'll do the same."

They parted ways, but as Tristan carried me toward the infirmary, other hunters whispered as we passed by. Tristan only held me tighter and lowered his voice to say, "Don't worry, Piper. I got ya."

On one hand, it was really sweet of Tristan to look out for me. On the other, I felt like a total jerk for letting him take the heat for me when I did indeed let Marcus out. Unfortunately for both of us, I didn't have a choice. It was him, or me and mine. And while Tristan was a nice enough guy, I'd do worse than throw a maybe not so innocent guy under the proverbial bus to keep us safe.

Chapter 11

Allister

THIS WAS SUCH BULLSHIT. How could she do this to us? It wasn't like we didn't have enough to worry about with the hunters chasing us and Marcus's capture. Why not go undercover into the only place more dangerous than being on the run? Yeah, that was a great idea. Good job, Piper.

"Man, can you like cool it for five minutes?" Rayne rubbed his temples, his elbows on his knees as he squeezed his eyes closed. "You are giving me a serious migraine."

"Then stop listening." I pushed off the windowsill of the hotel room Darren had rented for him and Piper. We'd arrived shortly after Gretchen told us where Piper had gone with Darren. The fact that it was in Atlanta had been dumb luck. Any farther, and we would have been in trouble.

Rayne opened his eyes and glared up at me. "I can't help it when you project so damn loudly."

"Well, I'm a little stressed. What do you expect?" My voice rose an octave, pulling the attention of my brother who was busy going over the map of the manor Piper had gone into. He arched his brow at me, but I ignored him, choosing to direct my anger and frustration at Rayne.

Rayne stood up and shoved a finger at my chest. "We're all stressed. It's not just you." He gestured wildly toward the butler. "Darren over there is this close to a heart attack because he's stressing so much about Piper—
who he let go on this asinine mission by herself." He gave the butler a pointed look before going to Wynn. "Wynn might look like he's all calm lounging on the bed like the

world's laziest ass vampire, but right now he's going over every single thing he's said and heard from Piper during his visit, wondering if he missed something. Something that could have kept her from going."

Wynn shifted uncomfortably on the bed but didn't protest.

"And your brother..." Rayne swiveled his finger over to Drake and laughed mockingly. "Your brother is so freaked out, the only thing he can think about is pulling the heads off of every single vampire hunter who dared to look in Piper's direction. Like little flies." He made a deranged face as he pretended to pull the wings off of flies. When he was finished making fun of my brother, who looked two seconds away from pulling Rayne's head off, he turned to Antoine. However, before he could get a word out, Antoine must have thought something at Rayne because he snapped his mouth shut and twisted back around to me.

"You are not the only one worried about Piper. You're not the only one who loves her. So don't think that you can go off halfcocked on your own. This won't work unless we're all in it together."

I went to argue, but once again Antoine interrupted.

"Allister, Rayne's right." Our head of house stared down at the map of the manor on the tablet, not looking in my direction. "Piper went in there with a plan, and we need to make sure she can complete it without her getting killed in the process."

I swallowed my words and nodded stiffly.

Drake gave me a look, asking in his twin way if I was alright. I nodded again, less tight, and settled at the table they were at. The blueprints of the manor weren't easy to find. The vampire hunters really didn't want anyone to know where they lived or what was in it. We had to pull every connection we had to find these and then some. We were racking up debts with Morpheus, ones that none of us wanted to pay.

"So, have you heard from Piper at all?" Drake asked Darren, who shook his head sadly.

"No, but she's only been in for a couple of days. We didn't plan to meet up again until tomorrow," Darren answered in a monotone voice, as if he couldn't stand to put any emotion behind his tone without breaking. I'd never seen the serious butler so distraught before. It made this all the worse.

"That means nothing." I sighed, leaning forward on my hand, my elbow on the table.

"She could be fine, or she could have already been killed."

"No." The confidence in Antoine's voice made me feel slightly better, but only slightly. "If she were, I'd know it." His pale eyes focused hard on the tablet before him, his jaw tightening, the only sign that he was feeling anything.

"Well, then that means something at least." Drake snorted and scrubbed a hand over his jaw. "She's not dead, but that doesn't mean they don't have her already. They could be waiting to use her to get the rest of us. They currently have Marcus, it's only a matter of time before they get the rest of us."

I clamped my hand down on Drake's shoulder. He snapped his mouth shut and glanced over at me, real fear in his eyes. "It's going to be okay. We'll get through this. We've been through worse."

Drake drew in a deep breath, more for the calming effects than the actual need to breathe, and set his hand on mine, giving it a tight squeeze. "You're right. You're right. We can do this. We just have to figure out a way to communicate with her. Then maybe we can work out a plan to get Marcus and her out of there."

"Does she even know Marcus is in there?" Rayne inquired behind me. "I mean, we can't plan anything until we know the whole situation. Suppose she doesn't know he's in there. She won't know to help him and then it could be too late. Or suppose she does know." He paced back and forth, running his fingers through the long strands on top of his head. "Would she come back here to consult with you before making a plan to break him out herself?" Rayne gave a hopeful look to Darren before scoffing a laugh. "What am I saying? Of course she wouldn't."

We all laughed slightly at that.

Smiling down at the table, I commented, "Piper does whatever the fuck she wants, without asking permission."

"A fault and a blessing it seems."

All of our heads jerked up to see Marcus in the doorway of the hotel room.

"Holy shit, man!" Drake jumped out of his seat and barreled up to Marcus, grabbing him in a tight embrace without asking before Marcus rolled his eyes and pushed him away.

I walked up to him and shook his hand, nodding in camaraderie. "You don't look bad for a dead guy."

Marcus chuckled. He actually chuckled. Something bad must have happened in there for him to be acting this way, but now wasn't the time to be asking.

Wynn didn't move from the bed, giving Marcus a two-finger wave.

Antoine stood from the table as Marcus moved farther into the room. Marcus stopped before Antoine and they had some kind of silent conversation before they clasped each other's forearms and hugged briefly. Except when Marcus pulled back, Antoine jerked him close, sniffing him before scowling. "Why do you smell like Piper's blood?"

Everyone in the room but Darren inhaled deeply. The sweet scent of Piper's blood was all over Marcus, and it was pulling at every bit of the alpha protectiveness inside me. Piper could be hurt right now. Dying, or worse, Marcus might have killed her. It wasn't a secret that he didn't like her. That he wanted to get rid of her from the beginning.

Rayne must have read my thoughts, because he was stomping across the room and shoving at Marcus's chest. "What did you do to her? Did you kill her? Did you?" He hit him again and again before Antoine grabbed him by the back of the shirt and threw him halfway across the room.

"Calm yourself, Rayne. Let Marcus explain."

"Yeah, Rayne." Drake smirked in the redhead's direction. "You're the mind reader, don't jump to conclusions."

Marcus dusted himself off. Not that it did much good. His clothes were ripped and covered in blood. His and Piper's. He looked far better than he should for a guy who hadn't eaten in several days, and had likely been tortured for over half of that. But unlike Rayne, I didn't attack him. I gave him the chance to get his bearings before he finally spoke.

"Piper is alive." The room seemed to sag at his words, or maybe that was just me. That was until he added on, "At least she was when I left her."

"What do you mean when you left her?" Rayne snarled, coming at him again, but this time I stepped in front of him, holding him back from Marcus. "You just left her there? Huh? You took what you needed and ran? You coward!"

Marcus snorted. "Before you get your panties any further into a bind, you should know I can't make Piper do anything she doesn't want to do. She stayed behind by choice."

"Of course she did." Drake threw his head back and turned his back on the lot of us as if he couldn't stand to look at any of us right now.

Antoine placed a hand on Marcus's shoulder and then gestured to Darren who went to the blood cooler. "Sit. Eat. Explain."

Marcus took Antoine's seat at the table and accepted the blood bag. He sucked it down a lot slower than expected, but I had a feeling that might have been due to Piper's blood that lingered on him.

We waited anxiously for him to collect himself, but it was my brother who gave in first. "Come on, the anticipation is killing me. Just tell us what happened already."

Marcus sat the blood bag down on the table, completely drained, and crossed his arms over his chest. "The plan didn't go the way we expected. They were waiting for me when I rounded back to follow them." His eyes darted to Antoine, who inclined his head in understanding. "They drugged me, took me to a base, but I didn't get a chance to check it out before they were moving me again." He paused for a moment, collecting his thoughts. "The next time I woke up, Piper was standing over me with another hunter." Twisting in his seat, he narrowed his eyes on Darren. "She's bulked up over this last year."

Darren didn't even flinch, simply stared back at him, not giving an inch.

Rayne sighed with aggravation. "We know."

"She's pretty handy with a dagger too," Marcus pointed out with a bit of a smirk. It made me curious about what she'd done to put that look on his face.

"We *know*." Rayne scowled. "Just tell us what happened already."

Antoine shot Rayne a warning look before jerking his head toward Marcus. "Go ahead."

Marcus shifted back in his seat. "I was beaten badly and blood starved."

"You attacked her, didn't you?" Rayne snapped, before Marcus could finish his explanation.

"Rayne. One more word..." Antoine's command sunk into each of us, making the room heavier with tension.

Rayne pressed his lips tightly together and collapsed on the nearby bed, pouting like a child.

Marcus wasn't deterred by Rayne's interruptions or accusations. "She should have just left me there. I was as good as dead anyway." His lips ticked up at the edges. "But of course she wouldn't. She fed me..." He trailed off, saying more by not saying anything. "But when we were going to leave, she wouldn't come with me." Marcus shook his head, annoyance and a hint of pride on his face. "Pfft, she even cut her arm and made me bite her again to make it look like she'd been attacked rather than rescuing me."

"Why didn't she come with you?" I asked quietly. "Why would she stay behind?"

It was Darren who answered. Not Marcus.

"She doesn't want to just save one of you." All eyes turned toward the butler. "Piper plans to save all of you. Either by killing all the hunters or finding someone else for them to chase."

"Something else to chase?" Drake mused, his fingers tapping on the top of the table. "What the hell is that crazy woman thinking?"

"Don't let her hear that." Rayne snorted, then shot a look to Antoine to make sure it was alright to talk again. "She'll use those newfound skills on your balls."

I snorted. "Too late, they're already in her purse."

"Look who's talking? If she's got mine, she's got all of ours." Drake socked me in the arm.

I winced and rubbed the sore spot. "Good point."

"As titillating as this conversation is," Wynn groused from the bed, "I would like to know what we're going to do to get Piper out without getting her killed."

"Get her out?" Drake gaped. "After all the trouble she went through to get in? Plus, all the preparation she did just to make herself look the part?" He gestured toward Darren. "Didn't you tell him how many hours she spent training?" Drake rubbed his nose and leaned back in his chair, balancing on the legs. "She could kick our asses easily. The hunters don't stand a chance."

I kicked the side of the leg he balanced on, knocking the chair over. Drake jumped to his feet quickly, so as not to fall on his ass. He glared at me and I flipped him off. "Regardless of if she could kick their asses or not, we have to either help her or get her out." I glanced around the room. "I don't know about you guys, but I vote for the former. If Piper thinks she can get the hunters off our tails, then I think we should let her do it."

"I concur." Marcus leaned forward, just noticing the tablet with the map of the manor in front of him. "I didn't get to see much, but I do know one thing."

"What's that?" Darren stepped away from where he stood by the wall. His expression hopeful.

"The president of the vampire hunters is there now. That's why Piper was able to get in to save me. All the hunters were distracted here." He pointed at a large open building on the map. "They had some kind of gathering there. The president was going to talk to them and interrogate me." His words slowed as he thought of something. "Perhaps Piper could get rid of him or explain about...us."

"Do you think it will help?" Antoine inquired, leaning against the dresser.

"Killing him?" Marcus hummed. "Probably not. They'd just elect someone else."

"And convincing him otherwise?" Drake prompted, with as much hope as the rest of us were probably feeling.

A huff from Wynn drew our gazes. "If anyone could persuade this president to chase a more worthy quarry, it is our Piper."

Chapter 12

Piper

PRETENDING TO BE OUT for longer than a few minutes was torture. I had never been the most patient person. If it came to being eaten by a bear or playing dead, I'd be eaten seconds into it.

Tristan took me to the infirmary and before he could even lay me down, I started to get antsy. My nose itched. I was going to sneeze. I couldn't hold it back. It was coming. I couldn't...

ACHOO!

I jerked in Tristan's arm and groaned when I smacked my forehead on his chin. "Ow, fuck!"

Tristan's head whipped back and his arms dropped slightly before he held me tighter. "Well, at least you're not dead."

He sat me down on the nearby bed and stepped back. "So, are you really hurt or are they telling the truth?"

"What?" I held my head, my eyes squinting at I looked up at him. "What are you talking about?"

Tristan huffed and moved over to the door, shutting it quietly before coming back to kneel in front of me. "Did you help that vampire escape?"

I blinked. "Why would I do that? He fucking bit me." I gestured to the wound on my neck.

"But you're still alive. Breathing." Tristan sat back on his haunches. "You have to admit it's suspicious."

"What? Because the evil vampire didn't kill me, I must be in cahoots with him?" I shoved as much self-righteous anger into my glare as I could.

Tristan placed his hands on my arms. "I'm sorry. I'm sorry. I just...I don't know you that well and as much as I want to believe it, things just don't add up." He paused and looked me straight in the eyes. "Why were you even down there? I thought you were going to get a better look?"

I winced as he parroted my words back to me. "I know. I lied." I ducked my head and sighed, trying to find some way to explain without giving myself away. Thankfully at that moment someone came in the infirmary door. An old man in a white coat, who had to be the doctor, bustled in with a tablet in his hands.

"Ah, Mr. Parrish. What brings you in here? I thought I was told a young lady was hurt." The old man looked over the rim of his glasses, glancing between Tristan and me. "And you are?"

"Oh, hey, Doctor Colton." Tristan stood up and stepped away from me, putting some space between us. "This is Piper. She had a run-in with the captured vampire."

"Ah, yes. Miss..."

"Piper is fine," I told the doctor before he could ask. "And I'm fine, really."

"Nonsense. It's protocol for anyone who has been bitten to see the physician. We want to make sure you've haven't been enthralled." I held back a snort as he came to a stop before me.

Enthralled. Ha. A little late for that. I didn't need to be bitten by any of the Durands to be obsessed with them.

I sat still while the doctor poked and prodded at me. He checked my wound before pouring liquid on it that tingled, but that was it. Tristan and Doctor Colton seemed to sigh in relief when I didn't react. I guess I passed whatever test that had been, because the doctor worked on patching me up next.

"You're a lucky one. The vampire must have been in a hurry to have left you alive and not enthralled." The doctor seemed quite happy about it as he went about writing on his tablet.

I exchanged a look with Tristan, who seemed even more suspicious, and murmured, "Yeah, really lucky."

We sat in silence while Doctor Colton finished up his report and then shuffled to the back of the room. He returned with a medicine bottle and handed it to me. "Take these if the pain becomes too much and drink plenty of fluids. And no hunting." He gave me a pointed look and then to Tristan, said, "I mean it. You hunters think you're invincible because you're sturdier than the average human, but you're still mortal. You'll die just like the rest of us if you push it too hard."

I nodded but had no intention of doing what the doctor advised. I had a job to do and not much time left to do it.

Once the doctor left the room, Tristan moved back in front of me. "You let him go, didn't you?"

Staring down at the ground, I contemplated lying again, but Tristan didn't seem like the type to go running to the president to tattle on me. If he was, then I'd already be dead or worse, in Marcus's place.

Lifting my head, I stared him dead in the eye. "Yes."

Tristan turned his back on me. "Fuck. Fuck. Damn it, Piper." He spun around and glowered at me. "I put my neck out for you. If they find out you actually let him go and I defended you, they're going to think I had something to do with it too."

"I'm sorry, I had no choice." I kept my gaze on him, showing all the determination that I had to keep my guys safe.

Frowning tightly, Tristan grabbed a nearby chair and flipped it backward before sitting down. "Okay, okay. That's good. You were enthralled, but I don't know how we'd prove it with the holy water not working." Tristan rubbed his jawline, his eyes thoughtful. "Maybe the vampires have found a way around it?"

Tristan was close enough for me to touch, so I reached a hand out, placing it on his arm. Tristan stopped talking to look over at me. "No. I wasn't enthralled. I did it. I released him of my own free will." I sighed and shook my head sadly, hating to do this to what seemed like a good guy in every other aspect but the vampire hunter part. "I'm not here for the reason I said I was."

Those friendly eyes that had looked my way when I first stepped into the base hardened. His voice sliced through me with how cold it was. "What do you mean? Who are you?"

To my relief and terror, we were interrupted by Bishop. He didn't knock but barreled into the room with a victorious expression on his otherwise ugly face. I was happy that I'd been playing dead when he'd been carrying me, or I didn't think I could handle being touched by someone with a bad guy look to him. His nose was crooked from getting broken too many times, his ears were what they called cauliflowered from one too many hits to the head, and he had a snaggle tooth. His overall appearance put him just above Quasimodo, but several steps below Tristan, who wasn't even in the realm of my guys, which probably put me in a biased position when it came to beauty.

"The president wants to see you." Bishop crossed his arms over his chest and grinned wickedly down at me. "Now."

Exchanging a worried glance with Tristan who turned away from me, I released an annoyed sound and made a show of getting up from the bed. I grabbed the daggers Tristan had sat on the bed next to me and put them back in their sheaths, wincing at every action. If I was going to play the victim, I had to take it all the way. I almost blew it with Tristan, but I had a brief reprieve—as long as the president believed my story and didn't kill me on sight.

When I got close to him, Bishop tried to grab my arm, but I jerked away from him with a glare. "Don't touch me."

Bishop sniffed, then snickered. "You won't tell the boss no. None of them do."

I pushed past him to the open door. "Well, I'm not anyone."

This only made Bishop laughed harder. "That's what they all say."

We marched out of the infirmary, me in front, Bishop behind me, and Tristan bringing up the rear. I didn't know why he was coming. Especially if he didn't trust me now. Perhaps he thought that since he'd stuck up for me, that meant he had to keep playing along to keep his own head attached.

Either way, I was grateful. I didn't want to be alone with Bishop. He seemed the type to try and stick me before I could even get to the president just to spite me.

The hunters were all gathered in the common room, the scene so much like the first night I walked into the manor, except this time, where they mostly ignored me before, they all stared at me. Some were just curious looks. While others glared at me with open hostility. It seemed Bishop had been running his mouth since I'd been in the infirmary.

I felt as if I was walking down the gauntlet and I very might well be walking to my death, surrounded by enemies with none of my men in sight. A part of me wished I'd gone with Marcus while I had the chance. The other part needed to see this through. If I was meeting the president, this was my chance to plead my vampires' case. Or at least, maybe strike some kind of deal with him.

"Where are we going?" I slowed my steps to allow Bishop to take the lead as I realized I had no idea where the president was.

Bishop smirked and strode passed me. "This way, your lord and master is waiting."

I snorted, but my hands dropped to my daggers. Not grabbing them, but letting my fingers linger near them in case I needed to fight. I didn't touch my gun. Billy always advised me never to draw it unless I planned on using it. Daggers seemed like a safer bet if I needed to be quick.

Instead of heading into a different part of the house, Bishop led me toward the auditorium.

"Doesn't the president have an office?" I queried, my fingers twitching as things started to get worrisome. Or more so than they already were.

Bishop looked over his shoulder with a sneer. "You meet where the president wants to meet. He wants to meet in the auditorium. Be glad it's not beside an open grave."

My teeth gritted, my jaw tightening almost painfully. He had a point, but it still didn't make me feel any better about it.

The walk to the auditorium was long and painful. The only silver lining on the whole damn thing was the night was pretty. The stars shone down on us, the full moon lighting the pathway to my doom. Okay, I was being a bit dramatic, but still, it wasn't that far off.

Halfway there, I felt eyes on me. Eyes I couldn't see in the dark. I felt them on me like a caress on my skin and I wondered.

"Keep moving," Bishop called behind him, and I realized I'd stopped, staring off past the gates.

There was someone out there. One of my guys? I hoped and feared it was. I didn't want them to get hurt or ruin my only chance to fix this. Or worse, pull me out before I could accomplish anything.

Rayne? I pushed my thoughts toward where I felt the eyes. *If you're there, stay away. If you love me, you won't interfere.*

It was a shit thing to do, using his love for me against him, but I didn't know what else to do to keep him and the others from coming for me. I could do this. I had to do this. I wouldn't live my life on the run.

Begrudgingly, I caught up to Bishop, Tristan still on my heels. My footsteps slowed when the lights of the auditorium blinded me for a nanosecond. When my eyes adjusted to the light, I noticed the place was empty. The absence of people in the auditorium made it more intimidating and creepier than earlier that day when it boomed with squealing hunters.

"Ah, there she is."

My gaze jerked from the vacant seats to the stage, where a lone figure stood. His attractiveness could rival my men's. The dark curls on his head glistened from the product in his hair. An impish grin quirked his bow-shaped lips and a single dimple peeked out of his cheek. Shining diamond studs pierced both ears, giving him a boyish look. It was countered by the navy suit that could give Antoine's suits a run for their money. Overall, he did not look the part of what I expected for a vampire hunter leader. I'd expected something more in the leather Van Hellsing stock, not the billionaire playboy look.

Bishop stepped to the side of the stairs, moving to take a seat in the front row like he was waiting to watch a play unfold.

I stopped before the stage, unsure if I was supposed to meet him or wait here.

President Vincent stared at me, his eyes sliding up and down my form, but I couldn't tell if it was in appreciation or suspicion. The New Jersey accent that came with his words was no less shocking than the words themselves. "You must be Piper Billings. Maid and human servant of the master vampire, Antoine Durand. My name is Vincent. Please tell me why you have infiltrated our home."

Only one word formed in my mind. Fuck.

Chapter 13

Piper

I STARED IN HORROR at President Vincent. Tristan choked on air behind me and a quick look at Bishop told me this was old news to him. How he knew me was a mystery, but not one that needed to be solved right now. Currently, I was more worried about the man standing in front of me, holding all the cards.

Getting over my shock, I grabbed the handles of my daggers and narrowed my gaze on Vincent. "I suppose I should say it's an honor you know who I am, Mr. President."

His lips ticked up into a smirk, and Vincent waved his hands in front of him, a large gold ring on his right hand shining in the stage lights. "No need for such formalities, Piper. Call me Vincent."

"Fine, Vincent," I snarled with more venom than I meant to. "What now? Introductions are out of the way. Do we fight now?" I shot a cautionary glance around the still empty auditorium.

Vincent tucked his hands into his pockets and walked slowly to the edge of the stage. "If you would like. But I, myself, prefer the more civilized approach. At least, at first."

My brows rose to my hairline. "I apologize if I find that a little hard to believe. From what I've seen, you hunters are just as barbaric as the vampires you hunt."

A hand clamped down on my shoulder, and without looking to see who it was, I reached back and grabbed them by the wrist, twisting it and shifting to the side as Billy had taught me. Tristan gasped in pain, but I didn't release him, unsure if he was still on my side or not.

"There's no need for violence. No one here plans to harm you. At least not yet anyway. Besides, why would you attack the only hunter here who defended you? Bad form." Vincent shook his head and clicked his tongue.

With reluctance, I released Tristan and took a few steps back from him. I hated to admit it, but Vincent was right. That didn't stop me, however, from being cautious.

Turning back to Vincent, I decided I didn't like being talked down to. With the stairs too close to the smiling Bishop and pouting Tristan, I grabbed the edge of the stage and threw myself up and on to it.

With a small smile that was anything but pleasant, I crossed my arms over my chest and cocked a hip. "Now that we are on even ground, why don't you tell me what you want? If you know who I am, then you've probably figured out why I'm here."

Vincent scanned my defensive form and nodded in one swift movement. "I see no reason to go on with pretenses. We both know you're here to save your vampires, but for the life of me..." He huffed and moved his hands from his pockets to cross them over his chest, his fingers in his armpits as he thought. "I can't figure you out."

I furrowed my brow and then shrugged. "What's to figure out? You're attacking my guys who are the least dangerous vampires out there and I want it to stop."

A choking laugh came from Bishop, and he scoffed, "Least dangerous, my ass."

I turned my head slightly to face him, but didn't take my eyes off of Vincent. "Yes. If you hunters are such experts in vampires, then you would be able to figure out which ones are actually a danger to society and which are simply trying to live a semi-normal life."

Vincent threw his head back and laughed. "This is why I am so intrigued by you, Piper Billings." He ran a hand through his curls and shook his head as he began to pace. "You've only known about vampires for how long? Two years?" I jerked my head in agreement, not bothering to ask how he knew that. "And in that time, not only have you been able to ensnare one of the most prestigious and oldest families, but you have drawn the attention of an ancient. It's because of you we were able to take down Boris. And I believe it's you we owe thanks to for taking out Valentine, or I suppose your vampires are responsible. Either way, it was in response to their devotion to you."

I swallowed hard at the mention of Boris and Valentine, but put on a brave face. "I didn't do it for you. They were monsters." Ignoring the chortle coming from the peanut gallery, I glared at Vincent. "The kind of monsters you should be hunting. Not the Durands."

Vincent nodded thoughtfully. "Yes. Yes. I agree wholeheartedly. And that is why, Piper Billings..." He stopped before me and offered me a small smile. "I would like to offer you a deal."

I gaped at Vincent while Bishop jumped from his seat, cursing me and everything that was holy.

While I stared at the man in front of me, wondering if he had been hit in the head one too many times, Bishop threw the biggest hissy fit of the century.

"President, you can't be serious! She's vamp bait. She let one of our captives go and now you want to work with her?" Bishop added a few more expletives that even had my ears burning.

"Bishop." Vincent didn't even move his gaze away from mine. "Get out."

"But President—"

"Now." Vincent's gaze flicked to Bishop in a final warning before the man huffed in defeat and stomped as loudly as possible out of the auditorium. "Tristan."

"Yes, President?" There were fear and respect in Tristan's voice.

"Do you have anything to say?" He formed it as a question, but everyone in the room could tell it was more of a warning.

Tristan, being the smart guy he was, quickly replied, "Nope. Nothing. I follow your lead, always."

"Good." The smile returned to Vincent's lips as he returned his attention to me. "Now, can you tell me, Piper, why exactly all these vampires seem so intrigued with you?" He reached out and took a strand of my hair, which had fallen from my ponytail, and rubbed it between his fingers.

"Just lucky I guess." I smacked his hand away, earning me a teasing grin.

"Oh, I doubt that. You have a fire in you, Piper. Something I haven't seen in many of my hunters." He went back to pacing, speaking as if he were talking to a room full of people, or maybe he just liked to hear himself talk. "You went from broke and living in your car to the live-in maid and then to human servant. One would think you were enthralled by the vampires you serve—"

"I don't serve anyone," I interrupted him. "I'm not property. I get paid for a job and I do it."

"Very practical. I like that," Vincent mused, and then turned back to me. "That doesn't explain why you've decided to bed all six of them, including their ever-faithful butler."

"Well, have you seen them?" I retorted sarcastically.

Vincent cocked his head to the side. "So looks mean more to you than morality?"

I sneered at him. "Don't twist my words. My relationship with the Durands is my business and mine alone."

"Ah, not so alone I would think." Vincent winked.

It took me a moment to realize what he meant and I gasped.

At my startling realization, Vincent's eyes sparkled. "Oh, yes. I have eyes and ears everywhere. For instance, you thought we were oblivious of who you were when you snuck into our base." My shoulders hunched at that. "But I've had eyes on you from the beginning."

I twisted around to glare at Tristan, but he looked as surprised as me.

"Don't blame Tristan. He didn't know anything about it. They wouldn't be spies if everyone knew who they were." Vincent chuckled at his own joke. "No, I've had eyes on you for a while. It wasn't until Frankfurt that I realized how useful you might be to us."

I was beginning to piece together what exactly Vincent wanted from me and I didn't like it. Not at all.

Baring my teeth at him, I snarled, "I won't spy for you. I just want you to get off the Durands' case, and if I have to kill you to do it, I will."

Vincent shook his head, his hands up in a defensive gesture. "You have me completely wrong."

I withdrew my daggers and pointed one in his direction. "Then you better start getting to the point. I'm getting tired of this back and forth."

Vincent inclined his head. "Very well." Taking a deep breath, seeming to steel himself for what he was about to say to me, Vincent closed his eyes for a second and then opened them, a look of what I could only describe as a cat about to devour their prey filling his eyes.

"I want you."

I blinked. "Uh, what? Sorry, I'm taken. Like really taken. Besides, the fact that you're on the vampire hunter side and I'm shacking up with vampires is kind of a deal-breaker, don't you think?"

"No." Vincent's voice showed all the patience of a saint. "I mean, I want you to work for me."

I gripped my blades tighter. "I already told you no."

Vincent dismissed me with a wave of his hand like my denial was of no consequence. "You do not seem to understand the magnitude of your predicament." He held both hands up as if they were a scale. "You want me to call the hunt off on your men." The last word came out as if calling the Durands men was painful. "And I want to bring order back to the vampire world. It's a win-win."

Now I was stumped. How the hell did he expect me working for him would make that happen? I was only one person. He had a whole organization to do his bidding.

"Now, I know what you're thinking, why you? What could you give me that the thousands of hunters in my command couldn't?"

Vincent had me there.

He laced his fingers behind his back and rocked on his heels. "You have only been a human servant for a little over a year now, yes?" He didn't wait for me to agree or disagree before he continued, "And in that time, you have shown more dedication to your training than any of my hunters and have come further as well. I can assume those muscles and blades aren't just for show?"

My lips twisted to the side in a wicked smirk. "Would you like to find out?"

"See? That!" He clapped his hands together with childish glee. "That fire. I want that. You have the determination I need to actually make a difference in the vampire world."

I flipped my blades around until they were facing the floor and stood my ground. "What exactly are you proposing?"

"In exchange for keeping away from the Durands, with the contingent you can keep them in line." Vincent gave me a pointed look, before continuing, "I want you to use your vampire connections and human servant position to help us take down the worst of the worst."

I pulled my lower lip between my teeth and chewed on it as I thought over his words. "You mean, vampires like Boris?"

Vincent nodded eagerly. "Boris and others. The human trafficking ring that the Durands led us to in Frankfurt was the biggest break we've had in centuries." He held his arms open wide with a great, big fat grin on his face. "Can you imagine the good we could do with you as our inside woman?" He stepped closer to me and placed a hand on my shoulder. "Think of the innocent people you could save." Leaning forward, he lowered his voice to a whisper. "And all you have to do is say, yes."

I wanted to say yes. I did. In my gut, everything in me was saying wasn't this the very reason I stayed on with the Durands after I found out they were vampires? To make sure they didn't get out of line and kill anyone?

Except that was before I realized they didn't even do that. The guys only ever fed from paid donors or drank from donated blood containers. This would be me using the Durands to turn their friends and fellow vampires into the hunters. To go deeper into the vampire world than I already was.

Not something I could decide lightly.

On one hand, I'd be saving innocent people. On the other hand, I'd have to work with the vampire hunters, and since I would live as long as Antoine, that might be for the rest of my immortal life. Did I really want to spend the rest of my life playing spy? Possibly having to kill other vampires for these assholes?

Then, there was also the prospect of what if they're the bad guys? Sure, they killed Boris and took down that human farm back in Frankfurt, but that didn't mean they let the vampires who didn't prey on the innocent just go. Based on the way all of them had acted about the immortal beings, they obviously hated them with every fiber of their being. They couldn't or wouldn't just let them live their lives in peace.

And who was to say they would keep their word? What if one day they decided that I was too valuable an asset to let stay with the Durands, and then the next thing I know they have Antoine locked up and me out on a leash to make sure I did what they asked?

There were too many variables and not enough time to sift through them. After all, Vincent didn't seem the type of guy who would let me think about it. He'd want an answer now.

Taking a deep breath, I opened my mouth to give my answer, but before I could utter a word there was a commotion. It sounded like fighting and then a horde of hunters came pouring into the auditorium.

One of them, a woman with long dark hair, rushed up to Vincent and announced, "President, we have to get you to safety. We're under attack."

"By who?" Vincent asked, far less concerned with the intruders than with my answer.

The woman's eyes swung around to land on me. "The Durands."

Chapter 14

Drake

I HATED WAITING. AS a vampire, all we had was time, but waiting here in the car while Piper was in there right now possibly being tortured was the most agonizing thing I had ever had to endure.

"Worse than the time you and Allister got stuck entertaining the daughter of that bureaucrat with the high-pitched voice and hyena laugh?" Rayne questioned, a pair of binoculars up to his face as he tried to get some idea of what was happening inside.

I scowled but didn't reprimand the mind reader for dipping into my head. "Nothing was worse than Andrea, but close." I held my fingers up in a pinching motion. "Very close."

Allister shuddered next to me in the backseat of the car. "I still hear that voice in my dreams sometimes. Draconius, come tell me again how you single-handedly destroyed the fifteenth regiment at the Battle of Minorca." The mocking, high-pitched tone Allister said it in wasn't even close to how bad it had actually been. Nails on a chalkboard was more becoming than that woman's voice.

"Ugh," I rubbed my temple with my hand and leaned farther into my arm against the car door. "Please stop. It took me decades to get over that event and I don't need relapses."

Wynn chuckled on the other side of Allister. "If you think Andrea was horrid, you have not been alive long enough, my friend." He sighed and relaxed into his seat, his eyes drifting out of the window. "I once had to seduce the daughters of a local priest so he would stop preaching celibacy to the good townspeople."

"Oh, boo hoo." I scowled over at him. "So you had to dip your prick into something that wasn't your choice. Join the club."

Wynn's gaze turned to me. "They were a hunchback." My brother and I visibly shuddered.

"Not that bad," Rayne quipped from the front seat. "I've done worse."

Grabbing on to the back of Rayne's seat, Wynn added on, "Did I forget to mention they were conjoined twins with halitosis?"

Everyone in the car visibly quivered, even the stoic Marcus sitting in the driver's seat.

"What about you?" I bumped the back of Marcus's seat. "Who was the one person you wished you could forget?"

Marcus's dark eyes glanced up into the rearview mirror. "I am not chosen for my bedroom skills. All of my bedmates were by choice."

"Pfft." Rayne lowered his binoculars. "What about that—" He gagged as Marcus's hand wrapped around Rayne's throat, silencing him before he could get another word out.

"Don't."

The single word was enough for Rayne to jerk his head up and down before Marcus finally released him. Rubbing his neck, Rayne glowered at the massive man. "Geez, don't get your panties in a wad. It's not like I told them what you did with Piper." He ducked down, expecting Marcus to lash out at him again, but surprisingly, he didn't.

Since no one else in the car was going to ask, I decided to put my neck on the line. "What'd you do with Piper?"

"That's none of your concern," Marcus growled, his hands tightening on the steering wheel.

"Oh, come on." I kicked the back of his chair with my foot. "We've all fucked her. We all care about her. There's nothing you can say that would piss any of us off. Not unless you did something to hurt her." I paused, my gaze narrowing. "You didn't, did you?"

Marcus snorted in amusement. "Nothing she didn't beg me for."

I sighed in defeat and sank back in my chair. "Fine. Keep your secrets."

Tired of waiting, I pulled out my phone to find a game or something to play, but before I could begin a single match, Rayne cried out, "I see her!"

"What? Where?" All four of us reached for the binoculars at the same time, and it became a game of tug-a-war for a moment before Marcus jerked them out of our hands. Grunting with annoyance, I leaned over his shoulder and tried to see for myself. "What's going on? I can't see shit."

"She's leaving," Marcus rumbled, his gaze focused on what he saw.

"Is she alone? Is she in trouble?" Allister pushed in next to me, trying to see into the dark as well, but we were too far away.

"I cannot tell. She's being escorted by two other hunters. She doesn't look happy about it." Marcus lowered the binoculars and then dropped them into his empty seat as he dashed out of the vehicle.

We all grabbed for them, and then realized we could just follow him. With a similar duh moment, we raced from the vehicle to catch up with Marcus. He stopped by the fence, hiding behind some bushes. The yard was barely lit up by the night sky and we had to squint to see anything.

"Antoine should be here," Allister murmured beside me. "He's our leader. We shouldn't be doing this alone."

I placed a hand on my brother's shoulder to calm him. "We all agreed. If Antoine goes in there and dies, it's not only him, it's Piper and Darren. We don't need three dead bodies today." I smirked at him as I saw the other hunters loitering around the front door. "At least, not any that aren't hunters."

Before anyone could stop me, I jumped over the fence, darting in the direction Piper went in.

"Drake!" I heard my brother's voice quietly yelling for me from the other side of the gate. "Get back here."

I grinned and turned back, urging them to follow with two fingers.

My brother cursed, but he jumped the fence next. Then Marcus. Then Wynn. Only Rayne waited on the other side, arguing.

"Antoine is not going to like this. We're supposed to keep our distance until we're sure there's a problem."

I rolled my eyes and whispered back, "Don't be such a suck-up. We can't keep an eye on Piper if we can't see her. Now, are you going to get your ass over here or let us do all the saving?"

Rayne muttered, "Fuck," before he, too, jumped the fence.

I edged closer to the front of the house where two lone hunters stood smoking. My plan was to grab them and force them to tell us where Piper went. However, before I could initiate my plan, Marcus grabbed me, pulling me back into the shadows.

"What the hell?" I growled at him, jerking my arm from his grasp.

"Wait," Marcus ordered, and then a second later six more hunters exited the house and joined the others for a smoke.

My shoulders sagged. Marcus had just saved me from getting my ass kicked and us found out in the process.

"Do not make contact if unnecessary," Marcus reminded me, as he turned toward the back of the house. It wasn't the quickest way to where Piper had gone, but it would keep us from running into any other vampire hunters.

Quickly and quietly, we made our way around the house, keeping low so as not to be seen through the windows or by the surveillance cameras on the corners. When we got to the back of the house, there was a single hunter standing there talking on his phone.

"Yeah, Mom. I'm fine. Just getting settled in." There was a pause as he listened to his mom berate him about being nice to the other kids.

I mouthed the word, "Kid" to my brother, who shrugged his shoulders.

"Mom," the hunter drawled in an annoyed tone. "This isn't high school. I'm training to be a vampire hunter. Not make friends."

Marcus patted me on the shoulder and pointed toward the guy before doing some kind of weird hand gesture. Before I could figure out what exactly he planned to do, Marcus jumped the patio railing and hit the hunter—who, now that I really looked at him, couldn't have been more than sixteen—on the side of the neck, knocking him out cold. Catching the phone before it dropped to the patio, Marcus tossed it to Allister.

Without being told, Allister spoke into the receiver, his power causing the hair on my arms to rise. "Everything is fine. Your son had to go. He'll call you tomorrow." Without waiting to see if she was truly enthralled, Allister hung up and sat the phone next to the knocked-out kid.

With a scowl, Allister bumped Marcus on the shoulder with his own. "A little warning next time would be nice."

Marcus didn't seem fazed. "I did."

I shook my head and follow them with the others. "Whatever this is," I repeated the hand gesture, "did not include what you just did. I don't even know what that was."

Lifting a shoulder, Marcus continued without apologizing. Though, lifting his shoulder was about as much of an apology as you were going to get from him.

Moving around the other side of the house, we made our way toward a large area in the back. It was the only place that Piper could have gone unless she left the property.

Approaching the building, I noticed it was some auditorium of sorts. Sitting outside beneath the stars, its open top did nothing to shelter those inside against the elements. If we had been there for any other reason, I would have enjoyed exploring it. Perhaps seeing a show of some kind there, but I had a feeling the shows they had weren't the kind vampires would enjoy.

"Come on." Rayne smacked my arm with a knowing look. "I can hear Piper's thoughts coming from inside."

We moved in slowly, keeping to the shadows so as not to be seen. Inside the auditorium, it was empty. Mostly. Piper stood below the stage with two other hunters, and a fourth figure stood in the middle of the stage. The authority coming from the man and the way he was dressed suggested that he was someone of importance.

"The head of the vampire hunters," Rayne provided for us. We were too far away to hear what they were saying, but apparently not too far for Rayne to listen in to their minds.

"What could he want with Piper?" Wynn mused from his hiding place.

Rayne sucked in a tight breath. "He knows who she is."

"What?" I jolted and gripped the column next to me. "Then we have to get her out. He'll kill her for sure."

Marcus grunted. "Unlikely. Torture, yes. Killing would be too merciful for them."

"All the more reason to get her out of there," I reiterated, preparing to launch myself from my hiding place.

"No, wait." Rayne held his hand up. "I don't think he plans to do either." His brows furrowed as we watched Piper climb up onto the stage. They spoke some more and one of the hunters on the ground jumped up a few moments later, waving his arms wildly in the air.

"What? What's going on?" Allister hissed at Rayne, not liking this helpless feeling either.

"The president wants to make a deal with her." Rayne frowned tightly. "Something about trading our safety if she worked for them."

"What the fu—"

"Someone's coming!" Allister cut me off, shoving me to the side and back into the shadows.

If we had to breathe, this would be the time we would be holding our breath. As it was, we simply stayed quiet and waited for the hunter to pass by. When he was gone, we relaxed, turning back to the scene before us.

"What'd we miss?" I asked, anxiously watching the exchange. The president seemed more than thrilled to have Piper there, and even went so far as to get up close and personal with her, even with her blades drawn.

"Nothing much. Just talking her up. Trying to get her to be his spy for the organization." Rayne's brow furrowed. "He wants her to help him take out more vampires like Boris. Take out more of those human trafficking rings like in Frankfurt."

Marcus grunted. "Makes sense."

I gaped at him. "How can you even think—"

"Hey! You!" A shout rose up from behind us. We all turned at once, finding ourselves faced with a dozen or more hunters.

Lifting my hands, I cracked my knuckles and grinned. "This is it, boys. The final showdown. This will decide the fate of all we hold dear. Including Piper."

Allister groaned at me. "Way to state the obvious, brother. Can we please focus on not dying?" He shifted into a fighting stance as the hunters began to close in on us.

Not wanting to bring the fight to Piper, we moved out of the auditorium. There was more space outside to fight anyway. None of us liked to fight when we were backed into a corner.

No matter how much my brother detested my words, they'd been true. Our whole future, our lives, depended on this very moment. It was fight or die. While I didn't know about brothers, I didn't intend to go down without taking some of these bloodthirsty hunters down with me.

Chapter 15

Piper

MY HEART CAUGHT IN my throat at the sound of my vampires' name. Fear for their safety saturated my very core, but at the same time, my stomach quivered with anger.

They couldn't let me do this one thing, could they? They had to go and screw it all up. I was a grown-ass woman. I could go into a nest of vampire hunters without having them up my ass the whole time, expecting me to screw up. After all, it was me who saved Marcus. It was me who kept Rayne from having to take Morpheus's payment. I didn't see them doing anything useful this last year but running around in circles, except sometimes stopping by my house for a little hump and dump.

I was tired of not being in control. Tired of vampire politics and being in danger all the time. A small part of me just wanted to go back to my normal human life and forget all of this. But a bigger part of me, the part that was head over heels for the Durands, would break. I'd be irrevocably damaged for any other man and would likely end up drinking myself to death to stave off the loneliness.

Shaking away the dark thoughts, I pulled myself back into the present. Spinning from the president to take in the scene happening around me, I found myself in the middle of a big ass fight between the hunters and the Durands.

"Piper!" Drake shouted, as he dodged a hunter coming at him with a knife. "Come on, let's get out of here."

"Piper," Vincent's voice cooed in my ear. "You could end this all now. Just say yes."

My hands gripped the handles of my daggers as I struggled with what to do. He was like the devil whispering in my ear, which made me wonder where the fuck my angel was. I wouldn't be surprised if he had quit because of what a disaster I was.

"What the hell are you doing?" Allister called to me, fighting two different hunters at once while trying to see me. "We have to go now."

I searched the mob of bodies in the auditorium crowd and found a familiar dark head of hair. Wynn, even now, fought lazily as if it were all a big joke. How he was able to put in minimal effort while still winning was beyond me. He would always be a mystery to me. One that I planned to spend the next hundred years or so unraveling.

Shifting my gaze, I found Marcus. He, of course, had the most hunters surrounding him. Perhaps it was because they had already caught him before and wanted payback for his escape. Perhaps it was just because he was the biggest one there, but either way, Marcus was holding his own.

As I searched the crowd, I questioned myself briefly, wondering where Antoine was before settling my gaze on Rayne. Out of all the others, he was the fastest. Since he could anticipate their attacks, it was hard for the hunters to even make a scratch on him. The hunters fighting were getting agitated by this and were going at him full force.

They wouldn't last much longer. I could feel it. While I wanted nothing more than to pull myself from vampire politics and keep to my own little world, that wasn't going to happen. The only way I was going to keep these men in my life without fear was to make the deal.

"No!" Rayne knocked a hunter to the side and started for me, panic in his eyes. "Don't do it, Piper. You don't know what you're signing up for."

I pulled my lower lip between my teeth and shook my head at him, tears burning in my eyes, but I didn't dare let them fall. I had to be strong. I wasn't that klutzy woman who knocked over a priceless vase anymore. I had to face my problems head-on, not back away like a coward. That's what got me into this in the first place.

Besides, I had an eternity to figure out another way to save them. This was a bandage, a salve on a festering wound. If I could stop it, at least temporarily, then perhaps we could find another way. Maybe.

It was that promise of maybe that had me turning back to Vincent. He stood behind me with a bored expression on his face, the female hunter at his side. The hunter seemed poised to strike me at any moment. As if I posed a threat to her precious leader.

For a moment, I looked over the woman. She kept her long dark hair braided and out of the way, her dark eyes narrowed on me with growing suspicion and dislike. The pale olive color of her skin almost glowed from the moonlight beaming into the auditorium.

From her black combat boots to her crimson-colored pants that barely touched the hem of her tight-fitting black shirt and the large silver cross around her neck, every inch of her screamed badass hunter. Would this be me one day? Would my very being cause fear in humans and vampires alike? I held back a shudder. It was a scary thought.

"Mizuki," Vincent purred, placing a hand on her arm. "Stop glaring at our newest recruit. You'll scare her off before she even gets started."

My eyes snapped to his face. "I didn't say yes yet."

Vincent laughed. "Oh, but you are about to. I can see it in your eyes. You want this even if you hate it." My jaw tightened at his words, but I didn't argue with him. "You need something that doesn't revolve around being the Durands' lover."

"I'm not just—"

He clicked his tongue, interrupting me as he cocked his head to the side. "What are you if not that? Their maid? Their employee? Do you think you'd be happy with that for the next hundred or even thousand years?" I opened my mouth to argue. "And forget about keeping a human job. You're above that. Besides, do you really want to restart your life every twenty years or so to hide the fact that you don't age? Pfft. That's no way to live at all."

He had a point and I hated it. Ever since I'd begun falling for the Durands, I'd started questioning what I was to become. I couldn't be their maid forever. Darren may be happy with his position, but cleaning toilets and folding other people's laundry had never been my idea of a perfect life. The job was always meant to be temporary. I was supposed to be temporary, and now I'd bound myself to a vampire and everything felt oh so permanent.

While the battle raged on behind me, I dropped my daggers back into their sheaths. The sound they made as they slid home seemed more resounding than anything else in the room. As if with that very action, my fate was sealed. In a way, I suppose it was. I had, after all, just made a deal with the biggest evil in the room.

Locking my gaze with his, I lifted my chin and snapped out, "Deal."

With a glee-filled expression, Vincent clapped his hands together once and shouted, "Stop. The Durands are no longer to be hunted."

I shifted around to watch as all the hunters in the room immediately sheathed their weapons and stepped back from my vampires. Drake punched a guy, unable to stop himself mid-swing, making everyone flinch.

I pursed my lips and narrowed my gaze on him.

Drake shrugged, a lopsided grin on his face as he swiped blood from the corner of his mouth. "What?"

I shook my head at him and found Rayne. Out of all the vampires here, I knew he would understand my decision. I never wanted to be prey again. I never wanted to feel the icy breath of fear for myself or my loved ones on the back of my neck for as long as we all lived. This was the only way to make sure they stayed safe.

Rayne nodded in understanding, walking over to Wynn to check on him. The hunters filed down the aisle as if they were called by some beacon of light. My guys cautiously walked toward the stage, but kept their distance from the hunters. A hand clamped on my shoulder and startled me, and I turned my gaze up to Vincent's beaming face.

"My brothers and sisters, we have found ourselves a new ally." There was a mixture of cheers and grumbles at his words. That was fine. I wasn't here to make friends anyway. Vincent wasn't deterred by his mixed reception, if anything it spurred him on. "We have long fought against the plague of vampires, but now with our new allies," his gaze moved over my men as well, who straightened up at the attention, "we will now be able to clear out the bad seeds for good."

My throat tightened at his words, making me wonder if I had made a horribly wrong choice. I let my eyes flick over to Rayne to see if he could read Vincent's mind. When he saw me staring, he shook his head with a small smile.

I wasn't sure if that was a positive or a negative for the evil incarnate beside me, but I was going for hopeful. That was all I had, after all. Hope.

And a harem full of vampires.

Epilogue

Darren

THE ALARM NEXT TO the bed blared like a siren, alerting me to wake up. I groaned and rolled over, smacking the offending thing off before turning back over and wrapping my arm around the delectable creature lying in my bed.

Piper moaned and shifted farther into my embrace, her bottom wiggling against my morning hard-on.

A small smile teased at my lips. I placed my chin between her neck and ear and murmured, "If you keep doing that, you're going to be even later than you already are."

Piper grumbled something under her breath and shifted her hips against me again. I put my hand on her hip, sliding it down her leg before pulling it over my leg so she was spread out beside me. The tiny nightgown she wore slid up to her waist, revealing she had not replaced the underwear I'd torn off her last night.

I trailed my fingers up and down the inside of her thigh, teasing her but not giving her what she wanted, even though she tried to buck her hips to get it. "Piper, my darling, as much as I'd love to feed your addiction, you really must get up."

"No," Piper drawled, burying her face into her pillow once more. "Let someone else hunt tonight."

I nipped at her ear. "But Mizuki will be very disappointed to hear her favorite companion isn't coming with her on the nightly patrols."

She mumbled something into her pillow I couldn't hear.

"What was that?" I nudged her with my nose. "You want me to have Drake come wake you?"

Piper shot up in bed. "No!" Her eyes wide, she glared down at me. "Do not send that sadist in here. Last time he dumped a bucket of cold water on me. I had a cold for a week!"

I chuckled at her abhorrence, then watched her climb out of bed. Her nightgown slipped back down, covering up her delectable backside from my view. Ever since Piper had joined the vampire hunters in their nightly hunts, she'd been more reluctant to leave the house. Though, secretly, I think she loved it. She didn't seem as happy cleaning toilets as she did hunting down bad guys. Also, with her there to tell if they were actually the kind of vampires that preyed on the weak versus those who were simply trying to blend in with society, there was a lot less for the vampires to worry about. At least, the ones who knew about her.

President Vincent had strict orders for Piper to keep her identity a secret. The only vampires allowed to know who she worked for were ones she was going to kill or the Durands. So far it was going pretty well, but we were only a few months into it. Who knew what the future held for us?

"I don't know why he makes me go on these stupid patrols." Piper stepped out of the bathroom with her mouth full of toothpaste. "I'm supposed to be undercover not walking the streets with the common hunter. I mean, what's the point of it being a secret otherwise?" She ducked back into the bathroom where the faucet turned on as she rinsed.

"I believe the purpose is to keep your skills sharp. With the Durands not having any pressing social matters to attend to—their creator being dead and all—they have no use for your spying as of yet." I angled myself so I could see better into the bathroom. "Besides, the exercise is good for you. You shouldn't stay cooped up in this house every day."

Piper leaned back to peek out of the bathroom. "Are you trying to tell me something?" The way her brow arched in warning made me chuckle.

"Oh, no. I would never. You are perfect the way you are. However..." I slipped over to her side of the bed, letting my legs drop to the floor, the sheet covering my bare lower half. "I do think you enjoy it for all your complaining."

Piper smirked and sashayed across the room to stand in front of me. "You know what I do enjoy?" She slid one leg on either side of me, placing her hot core against my length. Leaning forward, she caught my ear between her teeth and tugged, grinding her hips against me. "You inside me."

I chuckled darkly, my own arousal flaring up. "Ah, ha, yes, I do enjoy that as well, but we have plenty of time to revisit that activity when you come back."

Piper pouted, blinking up at me from beneath her eyelashes. "But what if I don't come back? This could be the night where one of them gets me. Then you'll never have me again. Do you really want your last memory of me to be this?"

I cupped her ass in my hands and drew her tight against me, my length sliding against her warmth. "Guilt, Piper? Really? I thought you were above that."

Piper grinned mischievously. "Not when it comes to what I want."

"And what is that?" Antoine's voice came from the bedroom door, and the heat in it caused a delightful shiver down my spine. "Piper, aren't you supposed to be leaving?"

Piper tried to give Antoine the same puppy dog eyes, but our leader didn't quite break the same way the rest of us did with Piper. Either he was made of sterner stuff or he delighted in defying her.

"Stop trying to distract Darren and get your butt moving. You didn't go through all this trouble to mess up already, did you?"

Antoine hummed, arching a brow at our position. "Or do you think a quick fuck is worth all our lives?"

Antoine was the master of guilt. Piper didn't have a leg to stand on and she knew it.

With a huff, she slid from my lap, making me grunt at the movement. "Oh, alright. You don't got to do me like that. I was going already."

Antoine hummed once more. "Of course you were." We both watched her with attentive eyes as she walked around the room. Every time she had to get something from the floor, she bent over in a way that showed her wet folds. I licked my lips, my eyes moving over to Antoine. The bulge in his pants was evidence that he wasn't so in control of himself that the sight did not affect him. Perhaps, when Piper left, we could help each other relieve ourselves of our burdens.

As if reading my thoughts, Antoine's eyes shifted over to mine. His gaze skimmed over my face with a dark heat that had my length hardening even further. Those pale orbs dropped to my lap and his lips parted. I could practically feel his gaze on me, stroking along my heated skin, his cock pumping inside me. I was near bursting already just from the thought.

"Ugh, fuck." Piper scowled, holding up her bra. "Seriously, you guys need to stop ripping my clothes off. I'm running out of things to wear."

My lips curled up into a proud grin. "And waste the time unlatching it?"

Piper's eyes narrowed on me, and then focused on the tension between Antoine and me. "This is so not fair. I have to go hunt vampires and you two are going to fuck in my bed. So not fair."

I smirked. "We could do it on mine if you'd prefer."

Piper walked over to the bed, crawling halfway across to kiss me on the lips. "And miss out on recording it? Hell no." She pointed to the corner of the room where a small camera was mounted to the ceiling. "Remember to angle that way. Thanks." She kissed me again and headed for Antoine.

He didn't let her get away with a single peck on the lips. Antoine wrapped her up in his arms, one hand tight in her hair and the other clutching her ass, and he devoured her with his mouth until her knees grew weak and she had a dazed expression on her face when he finally released her.

I sighed and shook my head. He was such a competitive man. If we weren't lovers as well, I'd probably have a problem with it, but as it was, I always enjoyed letting him prove himself the better lover. After all, we had loads of time to practice.

"I'll see you when you get home." Antoine caressed the side of her face with a gentle smile.

"Oh?" Piper's expression perked up. "Do you have something planned?"

A wicked gleam sparked in Antoine's eyes that made me worry for Piper's sanity. It was never a good thing when he looked that way. Sliding his hand around to the back of her neck, he held her close as he murmured, "We still haven't discussed the extent of your punishment."

Piper's eyes widened. "Wha...what punishment?"

Antoine's gaze narrowed. "Did you really think you would get away with signing your life away?"

"But...but it was for you. I did it to save you!" Piper's eyes darted to me and then back to Antoine, pleading for my help. I lifted my hands to show her I was not getting into it.

"Don't look to him. Darren allowed you to go into enemy territory without telling me, so he will be participating as well." The heavy look Antoine gave me caused me to swallow thickly.

"B-But it's not bad, right?" Piper stuttered, her expression growing frantic. "It's just like extra chores or something, right?" Antoine didn't answer her, simply leading her to the bedroom door where he promptly closed it in her face and flicked the lock. Piper pounded on the door. "Come on, Antoine, don't make me spend all night guessing. That's gonna be torture."

"Then you better not think about it," Antoine replied, turning his back to the door with predatory gleam seeping into his expression as he started toward me. "Now, for you, my servant. I do believe a separate sort of punishment is required. Don't you think?"

I swallowed, my mouth dry, not from fear but anticipation. While Piper might fear Antoine's punishment, I knew my master well. This was not a punishment, but more of a reminder of who we belonged to. Something I encouraged him to remind me of as often and for as long as possible. After all, you could forget a lot of things when you lived forever.

About the Author

Erin Bedford is an otaku, recovering coffee addict, and Legend of Zelda fanatic. Her brain is so full of stories that need to be told that she must get them out or explode into a million screaming chibis. Obsessed with fairy tales and bad boys, she hasn't found a story she can't twist to match her deviant mind full of innuendos, snarky humor, and dream guys.

On the outside, she's a work from home mom and bookbinger. One the inside, she's a thirteen-year-old boy screaming to get out and tell you the pervy joke they found online. As an ex-computer programmer, she dreams of one day combining her love for writing and college credits to make the ultimate video game!

Until then, when she's not writing, Erin is devouring as many books as possible on her quest to have the biggest book gut of all time. She's written over thirty books, ranging from paranormal romance, urban fantasy, and even scifi romance.

Come chat me up!
www.erinbedford.com
Facebook.com/erinrbedford
twitter.com/erin_bedford

Don't forget to follow me on Goodreads, Pinterest, Instagram, and YouTube!

Want to be the first to know about my new releases?
Erinbedford.com/newsletter

www.ingramcontent.com/pod-product-compliance
Lightning Source LLC
Chambersburg PA
CBHW070944190726
48292CB00004B/1336